BRAVO WATCH

SAVANNAH'S FINEST SERIES

NICOLETTE JOHNSON

Bravo Watch

All Rights Reserved.

Copyright 2023 Nicolette Johnson

This is a work of fiction. Names, characters, businesses, places, events, locales, and incidents are either the products of the author's imagination or used in a fictitious manner. Any resemblance to actual persons, living or dead, or actual events is purely coincidental.

The opinions expressed in this manuscript are solely the opinions of the authors and do not represent the opinions or thoughts of the publisher. The author has represented and warranted full ownership and/or legal right to publish all the materials in this book.

This book may not be reproduced, transmitted, or stored in whole or in part by any means, including graphics, electronic, or mechanical without the express written consent of the publisher except in the case of brief quotations embodied in critical articles and reviews.

Day-N-Night Publishing

ISBN: 979-8-9852137-8-2

Library of Congress Control Number: 202391843

Cover Photo 2023 www.authornicolettejohnson.com. All rights reserved-used with permission.

Author Photo 2022 InterSeeding Shutters Imagery, LLC. All rights reserved-used with permission.

PRINTED IN THE UNITED STATES OF AMERICA

❦ Created with Vellum

She was unstoppable.

Not because she did not have

failures or doubts, but because

she continued on despite them.

—Beau Taplin

PRELUDE
CLARITY ROSE

FIFTEEN YEARS EARLIER...

I... can't... breathe, panting through every labored breath I take.

I can't breathe...

The walls caving, water seeping through the cracks...

Gasping for air—I can't breathe...

"Please," I beg as I scratch at my neck, feeling my skin split under my stiletto-cut nails, but I feel no pain.

I'm numb, pores on fire.

My clothes torn off my body with such force. My hands ripped from my neck and strapped to chains. My legs spread wide, bound with something I don't know, but so cold.

It's so dark...I can't see.

I smell their breath, filled with tar and whiskey. The stench making me gag, but nothing produces...

NICOLETTE JOHNSON

I feel my skin split under something so sharp I can barely feel the cool sensation.

Slice...

Slice...

Tear...

Tear...

Rip...

Rip...

Splinter...

The smell of my own blood takes me deeper into the darkened hole.

Flashes blind me, but the suffocation is what's unbearable.

The thick chain around my neck hurts so much. With every thrust comes suffocation. Stifling air stolen.

Every breath kidnapped.

Every breath labored.

I feel myself needing to drift but am forced to awaken with every excruciating thrust.

Flash and more flashes...

I see blurring figures surrounding me, touching me, groping me, taking every inch from me, every piece of my soul, stolen, and I'll never get it back...never.

TEN MONTHS LATER...

"Push! You must push..." the doctor encourages.

"If you don't push, she will die," the nurse pleads.

"Let her. I never wanted it...I never wanted her," I cry out, defeated.

"If you push now, you won't have to see her. I promise..." the doctor insists.

Sweat pouring down my face onto my chest. Tears spilling into my open mouth. The taste of salt and pain overwhelms my senses. I just want it to stop.

I need it to stop!

Moments later, I push, and I push, and I push, screaming at the top of my lungs; I push one last time...

So much pain; so much heartache.

I hear screeching noise, and I know it's here, the spawn of the devil himself.

"Please take her..." the nurse offers. "Hold her in your arms."

"I don't want to see, hold, or bond with her. Get her away from me," I cry to whoever will listen. "I don't want that thing," I cry out.

"Clarity..."

"No, keep her away from me. They did this to me. I never wanted to have her. You forced me...they forced me...now they can raise her. Get that thing and get the fuck out my room...."

PRELUDE CONTINUED...
KATHERINE HARRIS

PRESENT DAY

IT'S A FRIDAY, rainy and murky, to say the least. But, more importantly, my best friend and sister by another momma, Harper Bradshaw, has to face yet another exhausting and excruciating pivotal point in her life. Harper has to face her mom, who abandoned her as a child, her biological father, who was the worst piece of shit to grace this planet, and her brother, the devil's spawn himself, in court today.

This will be the first time she's met these people, and the only reason she's even going through this is because she was subpoenaed. Oh, she fought like hell to get out of this, but nope. Our luck is to torture us some more. Why not? It's only the story of our lives.

As I get dressed, I wonder why we have to encounter so much heartache in life to survive this soulless world. And to make things worse, her fiancé, Dominique Parker, has trial today for another case and could not be there to see her through this shit, so yes, she asked me to join her for support, and of course, I'll be there because there is no chance in hell, I'll let her face them alone, absolutely no way.

I decide to wear a navy-blue suit, a pink silk blouse, and black leather Nine West pumps. An outfit fitting for a time like this, and of course my momma's necklace. The only pendent, prize possession I have of hers. I never take it off. I look myself over in the floor-length mirror and approve of my appearance.

I text Harper letting her know I'm on my way, slide in the driver seat of my white Buick Enclave, and head downtown, where the fate of these three psychos will be determined.

"I don't think I can do this," Harper grit through panic breaths, twisting her fingers into knots to avoid walking through those doors. Doors so intimidating, it'll scare the biggest, the baddest of them all.

"I know this will be hard, but honey, you can do this. I know you have strength for this chapter in your life. Never underestimate your power, and getting up on that stand takes courage, strength, and bravery," I try to encourage her, taking her hands into mine, soothing the tension from her grip.

Taking a deep breath, "Yes, I got this! Thank you, Katie. I don't know what I would do without you.

"You'd probably be locked up for contempt of court," and we both burst out laughing like a gawd awful laugh in front of the courthouse in front of everyone. Yes, they probably think we're batshit crazy, but we don't give two shits what people think. This is our moment.

We enter the courtroom and sit about three rows from the front, waiting, anticipating the moment the three heartless assholes enter the courtroom.

NICOLETTE JOHNSON

Nothing else matters in this moment. Not the wedding Harper and I are planning for her next weekend, not my failed attempt at a relationship merely a year ago, and not the fact that I can't work with my best friend anymore because of all this shit.

I hold Harper's hand, grazing my fingers over her soft skin in an attempt to calm her as the doors open to allow MaryAnn Bradshaw, Richard Holmes, and Orangejello Holmes to enter and take their seats. But, instead, I feel Harper tense as her left leg bounces vigorously, her grip tightening around my fingers, and her breathing becomes soft yet fast pants.

"It's okay. You've got this," I whisper lightly in Harper's ear. "Breathe in, and exhale out," I continue softly. "That's it. I feel you relaxing your tension already."

MaryAnn glances our way, and for a split moment, I think I'm staring at my best friend. The resemblance is extraordinary. The saying, you look just like your mother, doesn't go unnoticed between these two. They could be identical twins, MaryAnn just an older and tiresome version of Harper.

Her sperm donor, well, he's a different story. His stern, firm jawline, fluffed with a salt and pepper beard, lips tight and creased with disdain. He's tall for an average man, built with firm, badger biceps. His eyes are so cold and black they appear to belong to the devil himself.

And her brother, well, he's pretty easy on the eyes, with a goofy yet manipulating look. His dreads, kept neat, too neat if you ask me for a person in jail. He's cocky like this day doesn't even phase him.

What a prick.

"All rise, the honorable Judge Tammy Amour, presiding. You may be seated," the Bailiff announces proudly.

We all stand and then take our seats when the judge enters and takes her seat. I've worked with Judge Amour on many cases. She's always been firm, but fair. And I like that about her.

"Your Honor, we would like to call the following case to order, two-two-zero-two-one-ten-five-four. We have Defendants MaryAnn Bradshaw, Richard Holmes, Sr., and Richard Holmes, Jr., each accused of ten counts of murder, twenty counts of aggravated assault, three counts of kidnapping, two counts of burglary, and sixty counts of possession of a controlled substance and distribution of a controlled substance," the Bailiff reads off.

"How do you plea?" Judge Amour asks.

"My defendant pleads guilty on all counts," MaryAnn's lawyer answers. That's right. But knowing the coward she is, she probably begged for a lesser sentence. What a piece of work.

"My defendant pleads not guilty on all counts," Richard, senior's lawyer, announces. Should have known.

"And my defendant pleads not guilty on all counts," Orangejello's lawyer announces.

What a fucking joke. They seriously gonna put Harper through a fucking trial, knowing she's going to break at any moment now. I shouldn't even be surprised.

"I'D LIKE TO CALL HARPER BRADSHAW TO THE STAND," THE District Attorney, Ms. Jillian Henry, announces to the courtroom a couple of hours later. Ms. Henry thought it would be best for Harper to go first, get it over with so she doesn't have to sit through the entire trial. Which works for us because I'm getting her hitched, soon.

Harper squeezes my hand before standing and proceeding to the stand. I mouth I love you, and she nods her head in acknowledgment.

"Please raise your right hand," the Bailiff instructs her. "Do you swear to tell the whole truth and nothing but the truth, so help you, God?" he asks as she places her left hand on the bible he presents to her.

"I do," she responds.

"You may take your seat," the Bailiff instructs, handing her a bottle of water.

"Ms. Bradshaw, may you state your name for the record," Ms. Henry asks.

"My name is Harper Bradshaw."

"How do you know the defendants?"

"MaryAnn is my mother, Richard Senior is my biological father and Richard Junior is my brother."

After introducing how she knows the defendants and why she's there, Harper explains her story in grave detail. And when I tell you her story is so unbelievably crushing, she had everyone crying in the courtroom.

Her testimony alone will end them, and that smug look Orangejello had on his face earlier has evaporated completely. Now in its place, a frown and utter fear pierce through him. Her father, though, not one single expression changed, and by that, we know he's the organizer, the puppeteer, the one who pulls all the strings…

"Ms. Bradshaw, you may step down," Judge Amour states with so much compassion in her tone.

That's my cue to catch Harper when she breaks because Lord knows, she will break, and I mean fall completely apart because that was the most, I ever heard Harper reveal about her childhood, parents, the death of her father, and all of the shit her family put her through and I know without a doubt, it crushed her.

We make it to my apartment to have a girls' night. Dominique is keeping Clementine and Lucas, their children, so Harper can focus on healing. The huge hurdle is over, and she made it to the finish line, a master at dealing with letdown, heartache, and despair.

"I want ice cream," Harper announces.

"Then, we'll get ice cream, binge-watch Beef on Netflix, and drink plenty of lemon drops," I add.

"Katie, that was incredibly hard, but I'm glad I found the strength to reveal my deepest fears, and I thank you because I would've never said any of it," Harper admits.

"Honey, I know, and you were a true badass up there, owning the courtroom with your truths. I'm so proud of you!"

I scoop ice cream into two bowls and add strawberry swirl with cherries on top. Harper's favorite.

We spend the rest of the day watching TV, laughing, dancing, and having fun like we used to. A time we will never forget…

CHAPTER ONE
KATHERINE

MY, my, my, the day has finally come! Harper, is gettin' hitched! This weekend is game day, and I'm so excited for her. Harper has been through so much, and she deserves to be happy. Unlike me, who probably should rot in the pits of hell with no return...

But enough about that...

I remember it like yesterday, Harper and the love of her life, Dominique, fought like cats and dogs, and now, they can't keep their hands off each other. Of course, they didn't know, but I heard them in the backseat of the car when we all went for a drink downtown, and I sure as hell won't spill the beans. She needed that pleasure, that carnal need. And she finally found it.

Now, two years later, and two kids later, Lucas, Dominique's son from a previous marriage, and Clementine, their adopted daughter, they really can have the happily ever after. Like, who finds a kid at a firehouse and is able to make her yours forever. You only see that in the movies. But, nope, not those two. They can make it into reality, literally.

I wish I hadn't...

No, Katie, you can't go down that road, not now.

It's a hot and muggy day in Savannah, Georgia. I honestly don't know how I do it. Working day in and day out, wearing this godawful polyester death trap they call a uniform. I really wish someone on the uniform committee would make changes and soon.

I'm in my apartment, which is located on the south side of Savannah. It's small, but it's perfect for me. Two bedrooms, an open and inviting living area, and a balcony, where I spend most of my time people-watching and drinking shots of Deleon, a tequila I found to be pleasant on the taste buds and rough on the aphrodisiac.

But not today, I have to work...ugh.

It's my first week back, and the captain decided to throw a wrench into Alpha Watch. Oh, there's still an Alpha, just not the same. I was on Delta Watch for a while, but it seems they need more women on Bravo, so here I am now, preparing myself mentally for what the future holds on Bravo Watch with some new blood. God, I wish I could transfer to anything but this depressing team. Hell, I wasn't even part of that shit last year, and now, I feel like I'm being punished. But whatever, I do my twelve and hit the door... nothing more and nothing less. The Special Victims Unit is looking for some new meat. Maybe, for once, I'll throw my name in the pot. What's the worst that could happen...

While putting my duty belt on, I turn the TV on to watch the news, really for the weather, because the honest truth is, I live the fucking news every waking moment of the day...

Missing girls here and there, a shooting on East 55th Street, and the City Council hashing it out again about some business wanting to open up on the Southside. Same old shit, just a different day.

I check myself in the full-length mirror near the door before heading out. I stay on the third floor, which is the top. Nothing fancy about my complex; just wish I had my own by now. I'm twenty-nine years old, and still, I find myself not living up to my potential. But no more. I vow to achieve goals I didn't think possible, make something of myself, and live the life meant for me. Then and only then will I open my shattered heart again.

I jump in my marked unit, turn on the A/C, and raise the volume of my music, allowing Coolio's Gangsta's Paradise to spread throughout the small space. Coolio's music does it for me every time, giving me life and strength to conquer the world one day at a time.

My phone rings, interrupting my playlist…story of my life.

"Harris here," I announce through the surround sound Bluetooth.

"Hey, Harris. This is Sgt. Maui from SVU. Do you have time to stop by my office? I would like to discuss something with you." Sgt. Maui is the supervisor of the Special Victims Unit. She has made incredible strides to ensure the safety of the weak and vulnerable.

"Sure. I'm headed to roll call, but I can stop by afterward. Does that work for you?"

"Yeah. My office is on the third floor of the Headquarters," she explains. "Oh, wait. We've moved. Totally forgot just that quick. We're now located at the Landmark building on Abercorn Street."

"Yes, ma'am. I know exactly where that is. I'll see you soon." We then disconnect. I wonder what that's about. Maybe a chance at becoming a Special Victim's Investigator…man, I can only hope.

My playlist switches to Bad and Boujee by the Migos, and just like that…I'm back in my zone…

CHAPTER TWO

JACKSON HENRY

"WHEN WILL you settle down with a nice young lady?" My mom questions as I make my way to roll call. Since I turned thirty, it's been nonstop of the twenty-one questions and randomly fixing me up with these debutants. I don't want an average-looking White girl. I want spice in my life, someone who will challenge me and give me something to look forward to daily.

Someone like Katie Harris. I had that with her, and of course, I fucked that up and honestly don't know how to make things right.

"Mom, please, with the marriage proposals. I'LL LET YOU KNOW when I see the right woman for me. But, until then, please back off a little," I state harsher than I intended to. She's just getting on my last nerve with these antics of hers.

"Sorry, honey. I just want what's best for you, and I'm not getting any younger. Between you and your sisters, I'm going to die of old age with no grandchildren," she states through sobs.

"Mom, I'm sorry. I didn't mean to upset you. I—I just. I have to head to work. Can we discuss this later, Mom?" I drop as I enter the squad room.

NICOLETTE JOHNSON

"Sure, honey. Whatever you say. I love you, son."

"I love you too, Mom."

We hang up, as I take my seat in roll call. We had so much going on last year Captain Sadie thought it necessary to split Alpha Watch up. So now, I've been on Bravo Watch for one year. Harper Bradshaw remained on Alpha Watch, Dominique Parker went to SIU, Sophia Martin went to SWAT, Victoria Morris went to SARIC, Gabriel Perez went to Charlie Watch, Katie Harris went to Delta Watch, and Noah Ethan...well, he's spending his time in his own personal hell right now.

Ethan caused so much pain throughout the department, but he's been making strives to correct his mistakes. I feel for what he's going through, but he can only blame himself. Trying to kill fellow officers because some psycho convinced you that's the only way to get your sister's back was poor judgment on his part. He had all of us to help him, and he chose the most ridiculous solution...terrorizing his fellow partners and best friend, Dominique Parker and Harper Bradshaw.

As Sgt. White begins roll call, Katie Harris comes strolling in, and I nearly fall backward out of my chair. What in the hell is she doing here? She's supposed to be on Delta Watch, not Bravo. I was on vacay for a week, and shit changed again. What gives?

But, you know what, this could be a very interesting plot twist. There is no way she can avoid me now. That uniform, forming around her curves, gun belt accentuating her hips, makes my dick twitch a little. Those captivating eyes and natural curly hair gets to me every time. I love a woman who doesn't mind wearing her natural beauty and look flawless and unnerved doing it. Still looking as sexy as can be with those suckable lips and baby making hips. My dick stirs even more just thinking of the ways I can bend her up and bounce on this dick. She sits next to the door, not really looking at anyone but her notebook. Sgt. White begins roll call, and when she gets to my name, I can see Katie's muscles tense in her shoulders, but she recovers quickly, never glancing up to meet my gaze.

"Here, Sarge."

"You'll be riding with Harris now that you're back." Damn! What are the fucking odds! I just might get my wish after all.

"10-4, ma'am."

"Um, Sgt. White, can I speak with you after roll call?" Katie asks.

"Sure. Is there anything else for the greater good of the shift?" Sgt. White asks and when no one responds, "Okay then. Be safe, be smart, and above all, watch each other's six."

As everyone stands, Katie and Sarge head to her office down the hall. Each watch has two sergeants sharing an office, except Sgt. White. She is the most senior sergeant in the precinct.

I stroll by like I'm not eve's dropping on their conversation when I hear my name. I freeze, unable to tear myself away from this apparent private conversation.

"Sarge, I can't ride with Henry," Katie complains.

"And why not?" Sgt. White asks. "But before you answer...make sure it's a damn good reason because I do not entertain the weak of heart. I know your previous sergeants were easygoing, but I'm not. I expect you to come to work on time, do your job, and be the best at your job, regardless of your past or your present. I'm here to condition you for your future. So, with that said, what are your complaints?" Sgt. White challenges Katie.

"Uh—I'd like to retract my previous statement," Katie states.

"I thought you'd see it my way," Sgt. White states smugly.

"Thank you for partnering me up with Corporal Henry. I know I'll learn a lot from him, and he will certainly challenge my mind," Katie states matter-of-factly.

"I didn't place you with him to challenge you. You have a gift Harris, and you don't even realize it. You will challenge him to be the best he can be. He's holding back, and I want you to reach within to help him release his hesitation. You can do this. I've seen you do it with Bradshaw," Sgt. White encourages.

"Yes, ma'am," Katie responds, but with more confidence. She stands taller, straightening her back and speaking with authority. She commands the room, something that drew me to her a year ago.

But damn, Sarge thinks I'm holding back? Am I really? I thought I was doing well with my arrests and numbers. I have the highest in the precinct. I guess not. At least this is my opportunity to make things right with Katie and Sgt. White.

Challenge accepted!

"Hey, Katie—"

"It's Corporal Harris," cutting me off with such a stern tone.

"Sorry, Cpl. Harris. Would you like to drive or sit shotgun?" I ask.

"Let's get something straight. I'm not here to be your best bud or play like this is something we want. I know you don't want to be my partner as much as I don't want to be yours. But the sergeant sees something in us, and I'm here to accomplish that goal, nothing more or nothing less. So, drop the pleasantries and put on your big-boy panties. We have a job to do. And, yes, I'll drive," taking the dangling keys from my arched finger. "It's my car after all."

Picking my jaw off the ground, we both manage to check over her vehicle because she has a take-home, and I don't. We both climb inside without saying a single word for the first twenty minutes until dispatch sends us on a missing person's report.

This is going to be harder than I thought.

I really fucked things up between us, and I have no idea how to fix it...

WE PULL UP TO THE ADDRESS OF THE MISSING PERSON. A frantic woman is pacing back and forth in front of the home, yelling at the phone.

"I'll speak with the mom if you can jot down everything, she says to me," Katie instructs, and when I don't answer right away, "You got that?"

"Yes, of course. I'll be your scribe," I state sarcastically.

"Look, you little—"

"Sorry, Katie—Cpl. Harris, whatever. I got it," I clarify. "I don't want to argue. Let's get this done and go on about our own business." And I see her shoulders slump with relief and satisfaction. One thing that can't happen is losing sarge's confidence in this setup. It's my last chance to prove my worth to this Watch.

We both step out of the vehicle, and Katie approaches first.

"Ma'am, I'm Corporal Harris, and this is Corporal Henry," Katie points to me. "We're here to help."

"They took her! Oh my God! They took my baby!" the woman cries out.

"Here, let's take a seat, and you can explain to me from the beginning," Katie states in such a soothing voice it calms both the woman and me. It's incredible how she does that. Maybe that's what Sgt. White was referring to.

"Okay. My name is Abigail Bactive, and my daughter is Emma Bactive. She's fourteen years old and will be fifteen soon. She texted me two hours ago that she was staying after school for band practice, so I didn't think anything of it. She always stays for band practice. But her Band

Teacher, Tasha Simple, called me a few minutes ago, stating that Emma wasn't in band practice. So that made me worried. You know," she states as she wipes her tears away. "I've tried calling, texting, and pinging her phone. But, unfortunately, her phone is turned off, and the last ping was four blocks from the school."

"Does she have any friends she might be with?" Katie asks.

"She has three friends, but two are missing already. They were labeled as runaways, but these girls are bright. They wouldn't just run away," Ms. Bactive assures Katie.

"When were the other two friends reported missing?" Katie asks.

"Three weeks ago. They've been on the news every night," Ms. Bactive explains.

"Right. I've seen clippings of them in roll call this past week," Katie states. "You said there were three friends. Where is the third?"

"I was calling her parents when you pulled up," Ms. Bactive clarifies.

"Okay, we'll make contact with them in a few. Do you have a recent picture of Emma?" Katie requests.

"Yes, ma'am. Just give me a minute. They're on my social media page," Ms. Bactive starts searching through her phone.

"Corporal Henry, can you get the photo? I have to get something out of the car," Katie asks as she walks away.

"Sure," I respond.

While she searches for the photo, I call the Special Victims Unit (SVU).

"Hey Mike, we have a missing girl, and we're pretty sure it's' pertaining to the other two missing girls y'all are looking for," I explain.

"Bet. Where are y'all now?" Mike asks.

"Forty-eight Alabama St on the eastside."

"We'll be there shortly."

I hang up with Michael Vegas in SVU and turn my focus back to Ms. Bactive. As I glance her way, Katie walks up and stops in mid-stride, staring at the photo Ms. Bactive provides from her social media page on her phone. It's almost like she sees a ghost. The photo Ms. Bactive provided is of four teenage girls as happy as can be. What could be so wrong with that?

"Corporal, are you okay?" I ask Katie. As if the moment never happened, she brushes it off and continues giving Ms. Bactive resources and information.

What in the world was that?

"Can you put the bolo out while I sit back in the car for a minute?" Katie asks a little flustered.

"Sure." She then walks away quickly. Something is seriously up. I've never seen her act like that before. "Ms. Bactive, what was Emma wearing when you last saw her?" I continue the questioning.

"She wore a white collared shirt, blue shorts, a pleated skirt, and brown Mary Jane shoes. Her hair is cut mid-length, bone straight, falling in her face. She was carrying her peach backpack," Ms. Bactive explains. "She plays the saxophone and clarinet."

"Thank you. All of this will help. Someone from the Special Victims Unit will be on their way. They will likely ask the same questions, but my partner and I will upload the picture you provided and her current clothing. We will also write a report. Here's a case report number with my and my partner's information. If you have any questions, please do not hesitate to ask," I explain as I hand her the CRN card.

"Please tell me you'll find my baby," Ms. Bactive cries out.

"We will do everything possible to find Emma and her friends."

"That's all I ask."

I then walk away and head to the patrol car.

"Are you okay? I know I'm the last person on earth that you want to talk to, but I'm a great listener," I ask Katie.

"You're right. You are the last person I want to talk to." She then puts the vehicle in drive and heads to Headquarters.

Wow, just wow, because nothing else can explain this blatant disrespect. Nothing.

CHAPTER THREE

KATHERINE

I WALK INTO HEADQUARTERS, leaving Jackson in the car. I can't with him right now. I can't deal with his shit and deal with this simultaneously. I just can't.

I head through a maze-like building called the Landmark Building. This is the new residence for the investigation division, the command staff offices, and the recruiting unit until Headquarters can get a much-needed makeover. I'm here to meet with Sgt. Maui and once I make my way through the perplexed hallway into a set of doors of SVU, I'm worn completely out. But I push through my emotions, my frustrations, my fears.

"Hi Ashley, can I speak with Sgt. Maui? She's expecting me."

"Sure, this way." I follow Ashley into the Sarge's office. Ashley is the Administrator Assistant for SVU. With a beautiful smile and lovable mood, she brightens me the moment I enter, something I really needed.

"Hi, Sgt. Maui, you wanted to see me?"

"Yes, please, have a seat," Sgt. Maui motions me to take a seat in her office. She has photos of her kids and husband on her desk. She has different motivational quotes spread throughout her walls, folders of cases piled up on her desk, and snacks and drinks for anyone to partake in. If I ever had an office, it would look just like this... "Katie, I've followed your work for the past five years. You have a way with people, victims, suspects, kids, women, and men. Something I'm looking for in this unit. I've watched your body-worn camera footage and read your reports. You're so detailed and passionate about helping so many people, and I know you would be a great asset to this unit," she explains.

"Are you asking me to join the Special Victims Unit?"

"Yes. That's what I'm saying. I want you to join my team, be a special victims investigator. What do you say?"

"Oh, God," I break, a wave of emotions scattering through me. I don't mean to show such a weak side of myself to the woman I look up to, but I can't control the waves of sensations tearing through my pores. Sergeant Maui embraces me with so much passion and heart while I cry my soul out... like a god-awful nasty cry.

"It's okay, Katie, let it out. I know you're holding in a lot and must let it out. Scream it out; yell it out. Break completely down and then hold your head high, show the world you got this, and prove to yourself that you will not fail."

And with that, I do exactly what she says. I stand tall and wipe the tears from my eyes. I got this.

Hold on...how does she know what I'm holding on to?

"It may take a while for the orders to be cut, but be ready when they are," she explains, interrupting my inner voice.

"Thank you so much for the opportunity. I will not disappoint you," pushing my inner thoughts to the side.

"I know!" And with that, I leave with pride, confidence, and a little sway in my step, holding my head high.

"Can we talk, Katie?" Jackson asks as I enter the patrol car.

"I'm not sure that's—"

"Stop! You keep doing that," he spits out, catching me off guard with such a forceful and demanding tone. Something I never witnessed from him or thought he could muster up.

"Doing what?"

"Shutting me out!"

"You left me no choice—"

"There's always a choice, Katie. I asked one question a year ago, and you never gave me a chance to even process the shit thrown into my lap. You ran and that was it. Nothing else to be said. You just dismissed me like a dead roach on the ground withering away. Can you imagine sitting at a table full of co-workers drinking and shootin' the shit, when all of a sudden your world turns upside down by a simple clipping of your girlfriend being fucked by not one, not two, not even three random dudes. Six Katie, six fucking dudes. And when I confronted you about it, your response is not an explanation. No, of course not a simple answer to my simple question. You chose to degrade my manhood. Do you even know what that feels like? Do you even care?"

"Yes, I cared, but you could have sided with me, listened to me—"

"How can I listen if you shut down. You assumed I believed what I saw. All I wanted from you was to hear your side. Give me some credit, for once," throwing his hands up. "You know what, fuck it. I don't give a damn anymore. Why should I? If you don't want to talk to me, then fine. Let's ride the rest of the shift in fucking silence, and I'll leave you the fuck alone. I'm sick of this shit. Fuck it all to hell!" he spits out in pure frustration.

Damn, he's really pissed at me, and he should be. I've been such an ass to him, and he doesn't deserve it. But I've never seen him like this before. He's always cool, calm, and collected. I'm the one who's out of control. Who says whatever comes out of her mouth, and the one who doesn't give two shits how I make a person feel. I'm the one.

Not him.

So, I do the only thing I can to make this somewhat right, I confess, "The video, it's me," I admit as we patrol the hot spots in our district. "I was raped repeatedly by several men, and that video depicts every excruciating moment I experienced that night. There, that's the truth. But I did not fuck my way to where I am. The Recruiting Unit took a chance on me, and I'm here to prove to them and me that I am more than that fucking video. Got it?" I blurt out because I so needed to tell someone. Anyone. God, these fucking rumors are heartless. How did they even find out about my past? How?

Fuck it, Katie, get your shit together, stand up tall, and fuck dem assholes. You owe them nothing!

"Thank you," is all he says, and for once in my life, I feel a huge weight lifted off my heart, my shoulders, and my soul.

I can breathe...again.

I'M IN MY APARTMENT, RUNNING A HOT, SOOTHING BUBBLE bath, stripping my uniform off, and tossing my duty belt in my closet.

Stalk naked, I walk into my kitchen to pour myself a glass of white wine and grab a bag of dill pickle Lay's chips. I then make my way back to my bathroom. It's not a vast area, but it's enough for me, with a stand-up shower in the corner, a garden-style tub, and a dual-sink granite-top counter. I have plenty of storage for my towels, washcloths, hand towels, and toiletries. There's a bay window, frosted, setting over the tub, and I dressed it with several scented candles. Just the smells take some of the stress away. Finally, I place my glass of wine on my makeshift side table and step into heaven, something I needed all day.

I slide into the bubbly water, allowing the piercing hot steam to soothe my aching muscles. Once completely engulfed, I close my eyes, and the scene from early replays on an excruciating loop.

That photo damn near brought me to my knees, and I tried so hard to recover without Ms. Bactive and Jackson noticing. At least, I hope they didn't see...

It was like an out-of-body experience, staring at my reflection in the mirror, but no, not my face—her face. It can't possibly be her. Her hair is cut short, with curly ringlets falling in her smooth dark face. Her skin is so shady and soft that it takes my breath away. Her eyes large, brown, and pure. Just like mine. And her lips...my God... her full lips can bring any man to his knees. I must've dreamt all of it because there is no way it's her...

She's smiling with three other girls, who are now missing. But not her...not my doppelgänger.

Tears seeping through my eyes, and of course, to torture myself some more, I replay that gut-wrenching night all over again...

I can't breathe...

I can't breathe...

Please, I beg as I scratch at my neck. I feel my skin split under my stiletto nails, but I feel no pain. Instead, I'm numb, pores on fire.

My hands are ripped from my neck and strapped to chains. My legs spread wide, bound with something I don't know.

I feel my skin split under something so sharp I can barely feel the cool sensation.

NICOLETTE JOHNSON

But I show no fear; no pain.

Slice...

Slice...

Tear...

Tear...

Rip...

Rip...

Splinter...

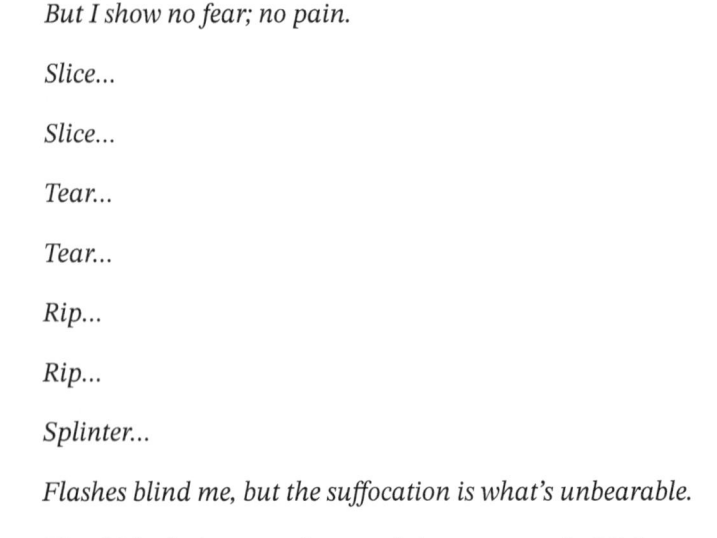

Flashes blind me, but the suffocation is what's unbearable.

The thick chain around my neck hurts so much. With every thrust comes suffocation. Stifling air stolen.

I peel my eyes open and run my hands idly over my body, counting each scar, bringing myself back to the now...1,2, 3,...10...15...40... and now, and only now, I can breathe.

You're okay, Katie. They can no longer hurt you...breathe in, exhale out...

I hear my phone ping with a message, but I don't bother to see who it is. Instead, I need a moment to gather myself, picking up each piece of my soul and putting it back together. I sip my wine; peach and white grapes flourish my senses with freshness and awakening.

I now have the mind space to wash myself, cleansing every inch of my body. As I caress my skin, I imagine Jackson running his calloused fingers over my body. He's never once questioned the many scars I have, and I'm so thankful for that, even though I need to be upfront and honest with him.

No wonder he doesn't trust me or him believing the rumors; I never allowed him to listen because I never spoke up or spoke out. Not even Harper knows the hell I've been through. Yeah, she knows I've been in foster home after foster home and had no choice but to become an exotic dancer at such a young age; but, I never gave her details of those isolated nights, the pain I suffered night after night.

I experienced heartbreak at a young age, five to be exact. I remember it like it was yesterday. My momma being slammed against the wall so hard; it literally knocked the life out of her. Then, my dad crying severely at what he had done to my momma, and even then, I couldn't shed a tear. My dad always hit my momma and was always remorseful afterward until he couldn't be anymore. He couldn't torture her anymore...he can't hurt her anymore.

I remember my momma doing my hair just like hers, tiny ringlets spread throughout, surround my round face; putting lip gloss on my lips, just like she did on her lips. She was so beautiful, not another woman could compare, with long think hair, loving dopy brown eyes and dark chocolate skin, melatonin so pure, so flawless, you'd think she was made from pure perfection. But no, my momma had flaws. She had a weakness beyond her control thriving from fear and feeding from terror.

I was too young to realize it then, but my momma's fate fell into my father's hands where he twisted her thoughts, crumbling her beauty day after day and destroying any chance of self awareness and self care.

I watched the police place my daddy in handcuffs and zip my momma in the blackest bag I've ever seen. I didn't know it then, but that very moment in time forced my fate to change forever...

Horrible family after horrible family until I chose to run, disappear and start over, to make something of myself... until that horrendous night...

Karma is a hateful bitch...

CHAPTER FOUR

JACKSON

I TEXT HER, and no response... not even those three f-ing dots. All day I've been stirring over that statement. How do you drop a ball like that and then just ghost me? How?

I'm sitting in my game room, my sanctuary, my refuge, playing FortNite to take the edge off. Nothing like drinking a cold one, feet propped up, and letting out some much-needed frustration.

Don't get me wrong, I'm not a true gamer or one of those dudes who play video games to avoid life's issues. It's just a stress reliever for me. Some people run, lift weights, or shop. I play Sims, FortNite, and Call of Duty.

After a couple of hours, I awaken to a ping from my phone, alerting me I have a message. I've passed three levels, gone through four beers and two shots of 1942, dozed off in my lazy boy, and now she wants to text me back.

Granted, I've waited all fucking day for this text, but still...

I open the message:

Katie: Hey, I know you have questions, and I know I have to answer them soon... I'm just not ready yet. Can you accept that?

Can I? The question lingers in the air, waiting for a reply. But can I be with someone who is so secretive about everything, someone who doesn't have a problem holding back, keeping things from me? Can I really be okay with that?

But... can I ignore the way she makes me feel, the way she makes me want to stand up and make moves, not allowing my parents to dictate every moment of my life down to the women I bring home or even want to marry someday, have children with eventually?

Katie is everything that my parents don't see in a woman. She's unpredictable, a badass, who is gorgeous, and fierce. But she's a shade darker than they will allow.

But I don't care how she looks; hell, I love my dark chocolate drop, with a little attitude and a lot of pizzazz. I want a chance to be with her again, make her happy, and give her everything she's ever dreamt about.

Who gives a fuck what my parents want? This is my life. I will live it the way I want to live it.

Jackson: Yes, I can accept that!

Upon request from my dearest mom, Bethany Henry, I'm in my childhood home. Anyone who knows my family knows my mom runs everything, and my dad, Jackson David Henry, just nods his head and beckons her calls.

Every Friday, at six in the evening sharp, we have family dinner, and when I say family dinner, my mom goes all out, like a Thanksgiving feast, so you can only imagine what the actual Thanksgiving, Easter, and Christmas dinners are like. Of course she has a cook, so she's not slaving over the stove. Hell, I don't think I've ever seen her in the kitchen. She probably has no idea where it is or what it looks like.

I have three sisters, Jamie, who left the moment she had an opportunity, Jillian, who's doing very well in the District Attorney's Office; and Jade, who married a rich man, William Bransome, and hasn't worked a moment of her life. Neither of them have kids, so dear ole mom thinks it's necessary to drive me up the walls with the baby talks. Jamie is the oldest, and when mom tried her matchmaking antics on her, she dipped quick. She's now running the largest Financial Firm in Atlanta. I couldn't be prouder of my sisters. They are doing the damn thing.

I enter the foyer, where my mom has a bar set up for drinks before dinner. All my sisters except for Jamie are here with their husband or boyfriend. I also see a woman about our age chatting and laughing with Jade's husband, William. She appears to be mixed with White and another authenticity I can't quite put my finger on. She has curly hair flowing down her back, virtually no makeup on and is very easy on the eyes, with legs as long as the eye can see, standing in three-inch heels with a short pleated floral dress. She's beautiful, but not as breathtakingly beautiful as Katie Harris. Now that fine dark skinned, mean as an ox, naturally curly short haired feisty woman, can take control of me any time she damn well please if only she gives me another chance…if only.

A guy can hope, right?

My parents make their grand appearance as the housekeeper announces dinner will be served. Impeccable timing, as always. Sometimes I wonder if they have secret bells stashed to let the help know when they'll grace us with their presence. One can only wonder.

We make our way into the dining room to our assigned sitting. Yes, assigned, because why the hell not. But as we enter, there's been a change. Yes, of course, I'm not sitting next to William. Instead, I'm placed next to the unknown female chatting it up with William. How the hell did I not know my mom would pull another one of her antics, after I specifically explained to her that I didn't want to be fixed up anymore.

Damnit mom. Now I have to play nice to this woman.

As she approaches the chair beside mine, she extends her hand to me, "Hi, I'm Claudia. It's nice to finally meet you. Your mom has told me so many wonderful things about you."

"I bet she has...." I state under my breath, taking her hand. "Has she now? Well, I guess I'm late to my own party." And she snickers at the statement. I don't find this funny at all.

Jade and Jillian trying their best not to burst out laughing.

"Aw, yes, I'm glad y'all had a chance to meet. No need for introductions," my mom states with enthusiasm in her tone.

"Yes, Mom. No need," I seethe, but she brushes it off like a gnat irritating her.

As we take our seats, Mom questions Claudia, putting her under the fire first. But it seems Claudia was prepared for my mom's antics because she answers every question without so much as a thought.

"So, Claudia, what do you do for a living," Jillian asks.

Thank God for my sister. Ask questions that really matter.

"Um, right now, I'm volunteering at Saint Vincent's Academy," Claudia responds.

"So, unemployed," Jillian fires back. And YES! There she is... the feisty fire I love so much. Thanks, sis.

"Volunteer work is very rewarding," Claudia offers.

"But does it pay the bills?" Jillian asks meekly or condescendingly. I can't tell of which by her tone.

"Well—"

"That's enough. Claudia is our guest. She isn't here to be interrogated," my mom interjects.

"Why is she here, Mom?" Jade steps into the conversation.

"Because she's my guest, and I can have anyone I damn well please at my house," my mom fires back.

"Oh, I didn't mean—"

"Claudia ignore them. This is a game they play with all our guests. But I won't stand for it tonight." And that shuts my sisters up.

"Sorry," Jillian and Jade mouth to me.

Shaking my head, "Don't worry about it," I mouth back.

The chef serves us our dinner, and we all eat in complete silence for about twenty minutes until my father breaks straight through the ice.

"Enough of this silence. Y'all are driving me crazy. I liked it better when y'all were bickering back and forth. Jackson, how's work?" my father starts.

"Work is work. We have a series of missing girls in the area, which is unusual for these girls," I answer.

"Why do you say that?" Claudia asks.

"They are all best friends and go to the same school. As a matter of fact, they attend Saint Vincent's Academy."

"What are the fucking odds," Jade states under her breath, only I could hear.

"I didn't know we had students missing," Claudia assures.

"And what, you thought the prestigious St. Vincent's Academy was going to let it be known that they have missing girls from their school, seriously," Jillian adds, rolling her eyes.

"No, I just. I'm sorry. I didn't know. But how do you know this?" Claudia turns to me.

"I'm a cop for Savannah PD. It's kinda my job to know when young girls go missing in our City."

"Oh, I didn't know you were a cop. I don't think Mrs. Bethany ever mentioned it." She turns to glance at my mom for an answer.

"Oh, honey. It must've slipped my mind," my mom responds.

Right, the games. All of the games my mom is playing right now.

"What exactly did my mom tell you?" I ask Claudia.

"Well—"

"Oh honey, there's no need to get into all of that," my mom cuts her off.

"Mom, I'm afraid it's the perfect time. And I would like to apologize to you, Claudia, because none of this is your fault." I turn to my mom with as much calmness as I can muster up. "Mom, you've got to stop this. I've told you time and time again I can find my own date, girlfriend, wife, whatever. I do not need you meddling in my private life. If I choose to bring someone home to undergo your scrutiny, then I will. But until then, I need you to back off." I then stand and leave without giving my mom another chance to respond.

She has got to stop this shit, and it needs to be now.

"How's it going, Ethan?"

Noah Ethan was a police officer a year ago with Savannah PD and best friends with Dominique, well, until he tried to kill Domonique and Harper. He spent six months in jail instead of life because he dimed Harper's family out. Apparently, her family was the real gangstas of Savannah that tried to terrorize anyone who encountered them. They were responsible for the City Market shooting only because

Domonique was dating the same girl, Dayna Pierce, as Harper's estranged brother, Richard Orangejello Holmes, Jr. Everyone called him Orangejello. He was a piece of work, beating Dayna, and when she tried to leave him, he had her killed during the City Market shooting, killing ten people in their wake to cover up the assault on Dayna Pierce. From what I've been told, she was a remarkable officer, helping children and women. She would have been a damn good Special Victims' Investigator. Instead, her life was taken too short, and to think she was pregnant with Dominique's child.

Dominique took what happened to him very hard, and if it wasn't for Harper, he'd probably be in a drunkin' stupper. Harper literally saved him and made it possible for Ethan not to face a life sentence with her heart-wrenching testimony in court.

"Nothing much, man. Same ole shit, just a different day," he states while letting me in his apartment. As I enter, I noticed there's been some changes in his apartment since the last time I've been here. His sofa is missing, and the coffee table and dining room set gone. His paintings are missing from the walls where they once gave life to the home. Now, what sits in its place, are blank white walls, a single lazy boy in the middle of the room, and a TV leaning against the wall.

"Dude, what happened to all of your stuff? Are you moving or something?" I question.

"Downsizing." The simple word given as if it explains everything.

"This ain't downsizing; this is repossession or eviction. Man, don't tell me they're evicting you?"

"No, moving with my mom and sisters until I can find a job. Remember, I'm fucking unemployed," he snaps.

"Whoa, I'm not the one that did this shit to you. So don't snap at me," I fire back.

Dropping in the lazy boy, with a beer in one hand and a remote in the other, "What can I say? I'm in a pissy mood."

"I've come to check on you, but if you want me to leave, I will."

"Naw, man. My bad. I'm just dealing with a lot."

"I know that. Have you found something yet?"

"No. No one wants to hire a convicted felon, especially an ex-con who was a cop. I might as well start robbing people."

"Or, start your own business," I suggest, because what the fuck? Robbing folks ain't the answer.

"And, par tell, would that be, huh?"

"Hell, I don't know. But it got to be better than robbing folks. And you need to talk to someone, anyone who can help. I know just the person who can help with your path. Sophia Martin. She's really good with a business mindset. She could really help you find your passion."

"Fuck no! She can't stand my Black ass; why the fuck would I even try?" he seethes. "Besides, being a cop is all I know. All I want to do, and now it's fucking gone."

"I don't know because I'm the only person who will put up with your sorry ass, well, besides your mommy and sisters."

"And what if she tosses me out just like everyone else?"

"Don't blame everyone else for your piss poor decisions. This is entirely your fault. And if you don't try, you'll never know," I spit out harsher than I wanted. "Listen, I got your back. But you have to want to help yourself. Stop feeling sorry for yourself. And start reaching out to the people you fucked and beg for forgiveness. Because if you don't, this will eat you alive."

"I know, man, I know."

This is the worst shit I've ever witnessed from a brother, a former cop. The depression is at a fucking high, and I gotta get him out of here and now. He's rotting away in this rut.

Well, not the worse I've seen... And that's why I need to be there for him. Help him through all of this shit.

"Let's get the hell out of here, have a drink, catch up. What say thee?"

"It's been a while; a drink at the Grove would take the edge off...But then, this little thing called broke, broke is preventing me from partaking in one of life's pleasures," he states sarcastically.

"Seriously, dude? I fucking know you're broke. I got you. I wouldn't invite a broke ass to drinks if I didn't," I clap back. What the fuck he thinks this is. "So, get your sorry ass up, and let's go!"

"Fine, dude. Give me five. I'll be out in a minute."

THE GROVE, WHAT CAN I SAY? WITH ITS SOPHISTICATED casual restaurant and rooftop bar in the heart of Savannah's bustling City Market, it's the very spot that makes all your frustrations disappear, if only for a moment. The lively music blaring around us, alluring us to enter its gates of heaven. The very young and middle-aged crowd sucks you into the hypnotic atmosphere.

As Ethan and I enter, we find two spots at the bar in an area you can people-watch and let loose. Something Ethan needs right now, with being two shades from erupted depression. I've witnessed this type of defeat before, and I'll be damned to lose another brother to suicide.

As we take our seats, the bartender, cute as fuck, with creamy pale skin and fiery red curls piled on top of her head, greets us with a sparkling smile. And if I hadn't had eyes for a certain dark-skinned, short, thick hellion, she'd probably be occupying my bed tonight.

"Hey, I'm Sissy, your bartender. What can I get you boys?" Sissy greets, placing a drink napkin in front of us.

"We'll take a shot of Don, and I'll take a grapefruit IPA on draft if you got it," I request.

"I'll have the same," Ethan states with a stern tone. Gotta dig him out of this rut and bring life back to his eyes.

The DJ's playing a variety of genres to liven the place up just a tab. As I scan the area, Victoria Morris, Gab Perez, and Sophia Martin come into view.

"Hey, look. Some of the old Alpha Watch is here," I bark over the music, waving them over.

"Fuck, I really don't need to be here. They fucking hate me, man," Ethan spits out, turning his body away from their view.

"No, they don't. If anything, they want to help you."

"I don't need their pity."

"No one pities you. Your sister's life was at stake. Could you have gone about things differently? Yeah. No question about it. But you must forgive yourself and fight like hell to regain Dom's and Harper's trust. And stop beating yourself up," I state firmly as Sissy brings us our drinks.

Gab, Victoria, and Sophia make it over and take the stools on the side of us.

"Hey guys, let's take that cove over there so we can sit together," Sophia suggests.

"Sure," I respond. "Just need to grab our drinks."

Ethan reluctantly walks over to the cove, and I order another round of shots for everyone.

As I gather all the shots and let Sissy know to keep the tab open, I hear Sophia talking to Ethan. And Gab and Victoria are in their own little world. See, I knew they didn't give a damn what he did last year. They only care about what he does to turn things around moving forward.

The only person missing is— and as I set the drinks on the table, I hear that melodic sound drift over the music. That voice brings me to my knees, literally, every time I hear it. There's no mistaking that sound, and I'll always hear it over anything.

My dick stirs just from the remembrance of our time together, a time I'll never get back. But, it's in the past; gotta live for the present to secure a moment for the future.

"Hey, bitches!" Katie shouts as she walks over to the cove. And as I stand and turn, I can see the panic in her eyes, but then it quickly switches to merciless. "What the fuck is he doing here?" she points past me towards Ethan.

Fuck. She's Harper's best friend. There's no way in hell she'll let last year go. Not one chance in hell.

"Katie, sweetie," Sophia begins.

"Fuck that. He tried to kill our partner. Are y'all seriously fucking kidding me right now?" Katie spits out with so much rage, shifting her gaze between each of us, landing it on me longer than the rest.

I stalk towards her, swiftly turning her on her feet and guiding her outside. "Katie, I know what you're about to say. But hear me out first," I plead with her.

"Fine," is all she says. So I better have a damn good response and fast.

"Ethan and I didn't know y'all were going to be here. We were at the bar when Gab, Victoria, and Sophia walked in. Sophia suggested we all sit together. Ethan wanted to leave, but I convinced him to stay and face his faults. If I'd known you would be here, we would have left. This is entirely my fault, and we'll leave if you want. But, just know. He's trying. He just needs us to be understanding of his flaws, huge ones, might I add."

"Harper and Dominique will be here any minute. What the fuck are we going to say to them?"

"Shit! I didn't know they were coming either. Wait—were y'all having a get-together without me?" just realizing the audacity of this shit show.

"Uh, no—I...fuck...," she responds, shaking her head and dropping her gaze to my feet. "This is my fault. Dom wanted you here, but I wasn't ready yet," she explains.

"Seriously?"

"I'm so sorry..."

"No, it's clear that you don't want us around. There are more bars we can partake from. Bye Kathrine," I deadpan, using her full name. Something I never did, but now...fuck this shit.

I turn on my heels, walk in, close my tab, and grab Ethan. "Hey man, let's get out of here. The Treehouse has damn good beer on tap," and Ethan couldn't be happier to leave this unwanted vibe that fucked both of our nights.

We walk past Katie, and I don't even glance her way. I fucking need to get laid and quick.

"I'm sorry, Jackson," I hear Katie whisper softly. Something I shouldn't be able to hear over the loud music, but I do, and I leave anyway, not acknowledging her apology or her sad gaze. I'm sick of being dicked around. Fuck her.

I AWAKEN THE FOLLOWING DAY WITH NOT ONLY ONE FEMALE IN my bed but two. Fuck, I can't remember a thing about what happened last night, but they got to leave now. I have to get ready for the wedding today.

Damn, my head is banging something fierce, but I gotta get these chicks out of my condo. And now.

So, I do the only thing I can do, wake their asses up.

"Hey," shaking them awake. They're both completely naked, draped across each other. One is a White female with blonde hair and perky tits with a skinny waist, and the other is a Black female with shoulder-length black hair, giant tits, and thick thighs. They're cute; they just gotta get the hell up out of here. "Hey, wake up," I shake them again. They both stir awake, and I tell them they have to go. Once they acknowledge what's happening, they dress while I make coffee. I pour them both a to-go cup and send them on their merrily way.

Did I pay to get my dick wet? Or are these respectable women who were looking for a good time? So many questions and not enough answers.

I can't believe I fucked two girls last night. I check my nightstand to make sure I wrapped up. God knows I don't need those types of problems.

Once I see the used condoms on the floor, a wave of relief washes over me.

Fuck, that was close.

The goal of last night was to cheer Ethan up, not get pissed, get fucking drunk, and bed two fucking broads. What the fuck was I thinking?

Oh, I know what I was thinking, fucking Katie fucking with my head, yet again. When will I fucking learn?

I jump in the shower, wash yesterday's frustrations away, and mentally prepare myself to deal with her all weekend for the wedding of the year…

Fuck my life! And this fucking hangover!

CHAPTER FIVE

KATHERINE

TODAY'S THE BIG DAY, and I must put on my game face. Harper needs me, and I'm gonna be there for her, no matter what!

She decided to have an evening wedding in Forsyth Park in front of the famous fountain and then have the reception behind the fountain underneath a clear tent with fairy lights, flowers, and LED clear balloons everywhere. It'll be breathtakingly beautiful, and she deserves to be a queen for the night.

After testifying three weeks ago, she needs to be pampered, if only for one night.

When she asked me to be her maid of honor, I jumped at the bit. She said I was the reason she and Dominique are together, and she wanted me to be by her side to witness their reunion.

Dominique chose his son and Jackson, my ex, to be his best men, probably because Ethan is still on our shit list. Serves him right with the dumb shit he did. Jackson reached out to him on several occasions to check on him and see how he was doing. Hell, he even hang out with him from time to time; explains why he showed up with him at the Grove last night.

Me, I don't give two shits how he's doing. He almost had my best friend killed.

I enter the Forsyth Mansion across from Forsyth Park. The inside is so stunning and remarkably detailed. It's one of Savannah's most treasured and historic hotels. Its intimate nature, with thriving art scenes, warm and welcoming, and such an urban experience the moment you step through the glass doors will take your breath away. But, of course, Harper didn't want to be too far from the venue when it was time to crash. So, she paid for everyone to stay in the Mansion's suites as well.

How could I say no to that?

The entry is so grand and magnificent. I see a courtyard when I enter, where most usually get married, but not Harper. She invited the entire department because of her lack of family. Some are coming to the wedding, but most are coming to the reception. It's the event of the year, and not one rich person will be there, well, except for Harper. She wanted everyone to feel the wealth, if only for one night.

The receptionist greets me and proceeds to guide me to my room when I bump into, no other than, Jackson.

Just perfect.

I thought I would be able to scathe by undetected until the I-do's began.

"Hey—" he pauses.

"Hey," I respond. This is so awkward. I despise awkwardness.

I start to walk around him when he grabs me by the wrist, halting me with just his touch, a touch that sends fire through my veins and erupts throughout my core. Oh, how I've missed his touch.

"Katie, please. Can we have a few minutes? Maybe a drink or coffee? Whatever. I just need a moment of your time," he pleads with me, feeling his gaze piercing the back of my head, begging me to turn around. But if I do, I won't be able to control myself.

And just as I suspect, he spins me around, forcing me to absorb his emerald stare, his blonde hair styled in a way that makes you want to run your fingers through it, and his tall and muscular statue, towering over me, commanding me, demanding me. Something he's always had over me. I can never deny him when he pleads with me in that panty-dropping seductive voice of his. Never.

God, I just want to lick him so badly.

Stop Katie, damnit! Keep it together. You have the power to resist his charm. You can do this. You have the strength.

"Please, Katie," he begs again, and that's all it takes to pierce straight through my wall. Imaginary bricks crashing to the floor, in a heap, at my feet. So much for restraint.

"Okay."

"Really?" he questions with hope in his tone. As if he didn't hear me correctly, or thought I would say no.

"Yes, I'll have a drink with you. Ma'am," I turn to face the receptionist. "Where is your bar?"

"It's right on the other side of this wall," she points with such an affectionate smile. "I can have your things brought to your room if you'd like?"

"Yes, please. I'll be at the bar for about an hour."

"Okay then. I'll make sure you're settled in your room. Here is your room key. If you need anything, please don't hesitate to ask."

"Thank you—uh,"

"Holly. My name is Holly."

"Thank you, Holly."

"You're most welcome."

NICOLETTE JOHNSON

I'm then guided to the bar in tote with Jackson behind me with his palm at the nape of my lower back. Never breaking connection, because if we do, I may just fall completely apart.

CHAPTER SIX

JACKSON

AND OF COURSE, my fucking willpower to just walk the fuck away evaporates the moment I see her. I can't let her go even if I fucked every woman in a hundred-mile radius.

If I'm going to go for it, this is my chance. She's finally giving me the green light, a moment I can't fuck up. A moment I'll never have again.

I guide her to the bar, pulling out her stool for her to sit. I then sit dangerously close to her, inhaling her scent, orchids of peaches, that smell that brings me down to my knees, every time. Fuck, I want her so bad. But not today or tonight. I have to show her that she means more to me than just a piece of ass.

She means everything to me.

The bartender greets us, "Hi, I'm Charlie. I'll be your bartender tonight. What can I get you?"

I motion for Katie to go first, "I'll take a raspberry lemon drop martini."

"And you, sir," Charlie asks.

"I'll take a Southbound on tap."

"Bet, coming right up." He then turns and goes to work making our drinks.

"So, you wanted to talk, so talk," Katie utters, impatiently.

"Right, straight to the point," pausing. I take a beat for a moment to gather my thoughts. "I want another chance. A chance to do it right this time. I messed up, no, I fucked up. I'm glad you opened up about the video," but before she can respond, Charlie serves us our drinks.

Right on time...

She damn near inhales hers and asks for another.

Fuck, that's not a good sign at all. I might as well take my loss and head upstairs to dress for the wedding. Being the best man and all. Have to stick to my civic duty. But, of course my body betrays me, not moving a single muscle. Just stuck to learn my fate.

"I—I," taking another pause. Because I seriously think she's about to have a panic attack if she doesn't. Something is eating at her, and I don't think it's the video. It's so much more, but I can't push her. I'll take whatever I can get, I just have to go at her pace. "I—I want to, I—I just—need, I need time. I'm not sure how much; I just do. I think we rushed things the first time...I mean..."

"Katie, love," taking her hand into mine. "I'm not trying to rush anything. I know there's a lot we need to discuss, and I betrayed your trust; and I want nothing more than to win back your trust, devote everything to us, make you feel everything. The way you react to my touch, the way your breath hitches slightly when I brush my thumb over your skin, the way you sigh when I kiss you on your neck, the way you make me feel when I'm inside of you, the way I make you feel when I pleasure every ounce of your body, the way you giggle when I make you laugh; I want all of that again. I need all of that again, and I know you do too. Just, please, one step at a time. Anything you need."

"Can I—Can I think about it? Give me twenty-four hours, and I promise I'll have an answer for you," she pleads. And just like that, I have no choice but to watch her stand up, take her drink, and walk away from me…

"WHAT CRAWLED UP YOUR ASS AND KILLED YOUR BEST FRIEND," Dominique questions as he gets dressed for his nuptials. I'm sitting, staring out the window, not really paying much attention to anything in particular. Katie got me all riled up. "Earth to Jackson," Dominique barks, pulling me out of my head.

"Not now, man. Besides, you're getting hitched. This day is about you."

"Fuck that shit. Something's up. Now spill the fucking beans, or you can explain to my bride-to-be that we're late because of you," he challenges me.

"Dude—"

"Don't dude me. Now talk."

"Fuck! It's Katie alright," I spit out.

"What happened? Did something happen?" alert in his tone. He's grown fond of Katie since she's his fiancé's best friend.

"No, nothing like that. Look, I basically begged her to give me another chance, and she damn near spit in my face. Saying she needs time and she'll give me an answer tomorrow, blah, blah, blah."

"Oh, I see."

"Yeah."

"You really like her, don't you?"

"Dude, like I told you before. She's everything to me. But she has to get over whatever is eating her up first."

"Then, give her the space," I look at him incredulously. "Hear me out. You're at a fucking wedding, with free pussy every fucking where.

Have a good time, and enjoy your night, if you know what I mean. If enjoying yourself doesn't piss her off, let her go."

"I can't do that to her," I confess as I help him into his tux. Harper chose a khaki linen suit with a soft pink bowtie and white collared shirt, accompanied with tan Stacy Adams.

"I didn't say it wasn't going to fucking eat you alive or feel weird as shit, but maybe this is the boost she needs to get her head out of her ass."

"Dude, I ain't never been the game-playin' type of dude. And this feels like playin' games."

"It might feel that way now, but you'll never know unless you go for it."

"I'll think about it," I agree to shut him up.

"That's all I'm saying. Now, can I go get my girl, or do I need to continue to be your counselor?" he jokes. God, how I wish I was this happy, marrying the love of my life...

What the fuck did I just say?

I ain't ready for no marriage. Nowhere near ready...

"Let's get you hitched!" Emphasis on YOU!

'Cause ain't no f-ing way Katie will ever walk down that aisle to marry a man like me... NO f-ing way...

CHAPTER SEVEN
KATHERINE

"OH MY GOSH, Harper, you look stunning. That dress, my goodness. The details," I gush. Harper's dress is made up of white baby feathers, hand stitched into a chiffon and sheer dress, with a tail so long, she'll need my help keeping it fanned out. But I'm up for the job.

"You think so? A SCAD student made it for me. You know I'm always supporting the local students," she states with so much admiration in her tone. "See how the feathers are more defined around the bust and then fan out down the length of the dress? It's incredible how she brought my vision to reality."

"Yes, I know," I state in a tone I don't recognize.

"Nope. Not today, Satan. What's wrong?" Shaking her head defiantly.

"Nothing's wrong."

"Bullshit! I call bullshit."

"No, this is your day. I have nothing going on, and that's my final answer."

"So, you just gonna lie to me? That's how we treat each other?" putting her hand on her hip.

"No, damnit. I just don't want to talk about it right now."

"And when has that answer ever stopped me from pulling shit out of your ass?"

Fuck! I wish she would just leave it alone. But she won't, unless I give her something; anything.

"It's Jackson."

"Yes, have you finally got your head out of your ass and fucked him already?"

"What?" completely speechless.

"Don't give me that shit. Once upon a time, someone threatened to kick my ass out their house if I didn't give a certain someone a chance…if memory serves me correctly."

"Seriously, that's a low blow, and you know it."

"Well, whatever works…" she deadpans, shrugging her shoulders.

"What the fuck do y'all want me to do?"

"Deal with your shit and let that sexy man fuck you into the middle of next week," she singsongs.

"It's harder than you think," I whisper oh so lightly.

"Look at me," she demands and after a few minutes of defiance, I glance into her piercing glacier eyes. "You're the most courageous, self-less, beautiful, and badass woman I know. I also know that you have a past, and you haven't told him or me everything, and that's fine. You don't have to share anything with me, but if you ever want what I have, then you have to open up completely. Be honest with yourself, with him. Because if you don't, you will lose him and you will have regrets. Jackson worships the ground you walk on. So, what! He wants to know more about you. That's his right if you're wanting a future with him. You have to give a little, and I bet you everything that he is ready to listen, to hear you, to understand you. But you have to take the first step. He put the ball in your court. Now, what are you going to do with it?"

My God, this girl right here sees me, can see straight through me, and that's why she's my friend. Hell, she's my only friend. The only person I really let in, further than anyone else, because I am terrified. Terrified of being let down, betrayed, and screwed over, like so many times before.

But she's right. I have to give him a chance and will give him that tonight.

I CRIED THE ENTIRE WEDDING. LIKE, A SNOT-RUNNING NOSE, tear-gushing cry. This was the most extraordinary thing I've ever witnessed. I've never been a part of a wedding, and to help my best friend join her partner, her better half, was such a glorious moment to be a part of, and I couldn't be happier.

After the I-do's and the crazy number of photos later, I help Harper pin up the tail of her dress to make her grand entrance into the twinkle-lit clear tent reception. It turned out to be a beautiful night. Not a single raindrop in the forecast. With a slight breeze and temps at calm, we couldn't have asked for a better night, if I asked personally from the weatherman himself.

"Katie, don't forget. You go get your man and be honest with him. You got this!" she encourages me.

"Yes!" I state proudly.

But, once we enter the tent and I pass Harper over to her hubby, Jackson avoids me like the plague. Like we didn't even talk just hours ago.

NICOLETTE JOHNSON

What the actual fuck?

I did tell him to give me twenty-four hours, but damn... Is he really stooping this low to give me what I asked for? *Seriously...*

I try not to make it evident that I'm seething inside, so I keep myself busy with making sure everything behind the scenes is taken care of, something I don't have to do, but if I stop, I might just lose my shit in front of all these people, cops, and family members.

I see Jackson dance with girl after girl, so close, they might as well head to his room. I've been asked a couple of times, but I refused, coming up with excuse after excuse because I don't want to dance with them. I want Jackson to ask. I want his hands all over my body and not those floozies. Fuck this shit! I can't take this anymore.

I grab a bottle of champagne and stalk over to Harper. I have to get out of here. I can't witness this anymore.

"Hey, sweetie, I don't mean to interrupt," I announce softly to Harper as I approach her and Dominique, giving me their undivided attention. "I'm not feeling well. Will you be okay if I cut out early?" I ask in desperation, hoping she just let me wallow in my own misery and she can finish enjoying her day, her special day.

"I'll be okay, but will you," she asks as she glances over to Jackson, understanding why I need to go.

"Yes, I'm positive. I'll ensure everything is ready for you and Dominique in the morning."

"Okay, honey, but don't let this discourage you. He's just hurting right now. So please don't hold this behavior against him."

"I won't," I lie. Because right now, I could murder him.

"Why don't I believe you?"

"Because you know me better than that?"

"That part. Go, I'll see you in the morning. I love you," she says as she embraces me in a tenderly hug.

"I love you too," and I actually mean it. I could never love anyone before, not even myself. But Harper is like a sister. She dove into my life with such force and now, nothing can separate us. Nothing. She means everything to me.

I duck out, take off my heels, and run and run some more, tears running down my face. I don't head towards the Mansion. Instead, I run through the park with the bottle of champagne in my hand and my heels and cell phone in the other.

I fucked up, and now, he doesn't want anything to do with me. Why would he want a basket case who's been tortured for pleasure, who's climbed a pole and given up the pussy for money, who had a killer for a father and momma so weak, she died, and to top it off, a person who would abandon her own child? Who would want me?

CHAPTER EIGHT

JACKSON

"HEY, DOMINIQUE. HAVE YOU SEEN KATIE?"

"Yeah, man. She left."

"What? When?" I question panicky, scanning the bar area, the dance floor, and the half empty tables.

"About ten minutes ago. I couldn't hear everything she said to Harper, but she was upset, didn't feel good, and needed to leave early. But, man, I think it worked. I think she saw you with those girls, and it pissed her off," he spurts with laughter in his tone, but this is no laughing matter. I'm fucking serious right now.

"But that's not what I was trying to do. I just didn't want to be rude to those girls. They know me from the academy. I tried to get to her all night, but she kept dipping out and helping with everything."

"She was making herself busy, so she didn't have to watch you with girls all over you, obviously."

"Shit! I have to find her," I'm such an idiot.

"Check the mansion. She might have gone to her room."

"Fuck, I never got her room number. Fuck, shit, goddamnit! Where's Harper?"

"Dude, calm down. We'll find her."

"Fuck that. I told you that shit was a bad idea. Now, for the second time, I've lost her."

"No, you haven't. We'll fix this. Harper, baby. Do you know where Katie is?" Dominique asks Harper as she approaches us.

"No, and if I did, I wouldn't tell your ass," pointing her finger at me.

"Harper, please? I need to find her, and I need to find her now," I beg.

"Why should I tell you anything? I stuck my neck out for you today, and you go do dumb shit like dry humping twats on the dance floor."

"That's not what I was doing. Damnit! I have to fix this now."

"Baby, please. Look on your phone and find her location. All of this shit is my fault. I gave him bad advice, and we gotta fix it," he tries to convince her.

"We don't have to do nothing. Y'all two idiots have too," Harper spits out.

"Listen, Harper, I love her, and I know I fucked up, but if she would give me the slightest chance, I promise you, I won't fuck it up again. I promise you."

After several seconds, a whole eye roll, and sucking of the teeth, Harper finally caves, "Fine, Lucas has my phone. We share locations."

"Oh, thank goodness," I breathe a sigh of relief.

"Don't thank me yet. Because if you so much as harm a hair on her head, I'll hunt you down and gut you myself. Do I make myself clear?" Harper deadpans.

"Crystal."

Dominique returns with the phone. Hell, I didn't even know he left. "Here, babe," handing over the phone to Harper.

She powers the phone up and then searches Katie's location. "It looks like she's moving south quickly through the park. If you sprint—" and I take off before she can even finish the sentence.

"Go get your girl!" I hear Dominique yell after me.

I continue running, my eyes scanning the park. She can be anywhere at this point, but I have faith she's around here somewhere.

I continue running when I hear something pop to the left of me near the tennis courts. Not a gunshot, but more like a bottle of champagne, maybe. I stop running but jog toward the sound. I then hear sobbing, and I know it's her.

I hear her yelling at someone or something, so I take off running again, fearing she may be hurt or attacked.

Once I get closer, it sounds like she's degrading herself. Saying words like, how can anyone love her? She's useless, has too much baggage, and abandoned someone.

Before I approach, I announce myself so I don't startle her. "Katie?"

"Who's there?" she questions, alertness in her tone.

"It's me, Jackson."

"Please, Jackson, just leave me alone. I'm not the girl for you. Never have been and never will be," she states in a depleted tone.

"Why do you keep saying that?" I continue to approach her.

"Because I'm damaged goods," she cries out.

"Wouldn't it be fair for me to make that judgment for myself?"

"Why? So, you can fucking leave me too? Hurt me too? Destroy every ounce of me, too?" she spurs out, taking a huge gulp of champagne.

"Is that what you think? That I'd leave you?"

"Duh! Y'all are all the same, fuck me then leave me."

"You really think I'd do that to you? You think that low of me?" Not a fucking word. Not one word spills from those soft plump lips. "Talk to me," I demand.

Taking another swig of the champagne, she starts crying again. So finally, I bend down and sit next to her, forcing her to let me wrap my arms around her and just hold her and let her cry it out.

After several moments, she begins with her story. And I just listen, learn, and understand the woman she is, who she wants to be, what she desires, and more. Whatever she needs from me, I'm here.

"Fifteen years ago, well, it starts a lot earlier than that," wiping tears from her cheeks. "When I was five, I watched my father beat my mom so bad he killed her. He literally slammed her against the wall, and the force of it killed her. When he was taken into custody, I was sent to foster care for about ten years of being beaten, molested, and tortured. Most of my foster families just wanted the money they were receiving from the government. Others decided to have families of their own and had no use for me anymore," pausing a moment to gather her wits.

"But there was one woman, Ms. Kathy Jones, who really cared for me, taking time out to guide me and strengthen me to be a better girl. She always said she saw potential in me. I didn't have a clue at the time of what that potential was she saw, but when she died, I suffered tremendously, leaving me to make the worst decision of my life. Trying to find just one family member who could take me in, but after being let down yet again, and to make things worse, I ran away and became a stripper in South Carolina," she continues.

"At the time, I had no idea what my future held because I was doing well for myself, finishing high school, and earning a little cash for myself, but then one night, a group of men came to the strip club for a bachelor's party. They wanted a private room, and I was selected as their night entertainment. At first, I was just dancing and having fun, but then they became handsy. Touching me, and grabbing me, and hurting me. They begged me to let them fuck me, and when I refused, they complained to the manager, and he basically told me if I didn't give them what they wanted, I was fired. I was fourteen and had nowhere to go, so I did it. I didn't know that they would tie me down, slice me up with razor blades, and rape me repeatedly for hours and hours. I was so defeated, broken, and torn by the end of it. I just wanted to die. And to make things even worse than that torture, nine months later at the age of fifteen, I gave birth to the product of that night. They passed a law in Georgia that women could no longer have abortions after twenty weeks, and I couldn't afford to go elsewhere. So, I had her and gave her up for adoption. I never seen her, nor did I want to. I just wanted to get rid of it all together. So, when that video surfaced, which I remember flashing, but I didn't know they recorded the whole thing, I relived that night all over again. And now these missing girls are coming up, and they're the same age as the baby I gave up…I just—it's too much," breaking down all over again.

"My God!"

"No, don't do that. Don't feel pity for me. I don't want your pity," she barks. "I don't deserve to be pitied."

"I don't feel pity. But Katie, have you been living with all this and never said anything to anyone?" I ask, genuinely concerned.

"No, why the hell would I?"

"Because it's eating you alive, and you have to let it all out…tell someone who can give you resources to overcome the trauma you've endured."

"I can't. I'm too embarrassed."

"Embarrassed?" I question incredulously. "You are a survivor. You should never be embarrassed for what those assholes did to you. The system failed you, and you have a right to claim your life back."

"I don't know if I can."

"You can, but only when you're ready."

"So, you don't hate me? I saw you with those other girls. They're better suited for you, you know. I'm damaged goods," she tries persuading me.

"Look at me, Katie," forcing her chin up so I can see into those dark brown eyes. "I care about you. I want you. I've tried to talk to you all night, but I didn't want to be rude to those girls. They know me from the academy, and I saw you helping out, so I didn't want to disturb you. Besides, you told me to wait, remember."

"Yeah, I know, but that was seriously dumb on my part. It really hurt to see you with those other women. I thought I finally pushed you away and deserved what I got."

"You can never push me away. Katie, you deserve to be happy, and I want to be the one to make you happy. If you'll let me. I love you Katie Harris."

I don't say those words because I expect them back from her. I say them because I've loved her ever since we met four years ago right here in Forsyth Park. She was utterly captivating then and she's even more gorgeous today. Katie takes every ounce of my being and then some. I'll always be hers whether she wants me or not.

She then puts the bottle down, straddles me, and places her palms on my cheeks. She glances deep into my eyes and does something I never thought she would ever do again. She kisses me fiercely, passionately, and she's so giving, and I take it all. Embracing her, taking everything she's giving me at this moment, and only going at the speed she wants to go.

And at this moment I realize I don't need to hear the words I crave so dearly. I know she feels the same way by showing me in her actions, her tenderness in moments like these. I know she loves me back.

After moments of kissing and touching, and feeling, she unzips my pants. But I stop her, "Are you sure? We do not have to do this tonight," I assure her. I'm not here to fuck her; I'm here to make her feel safe, feel comfortable, and feel anything she needs from me right now. Besides, I just fucked two chicks just last night. I can't possibly fuck her too, can I?

"I need to feel you, all of you. I miss you so much," fuck, how can I say no to that. I want to give her everything she wants, but I'm afraid she may be too intoxicated right now, anyways. Any excuse to calm my dick down. Because right now, everything is betraying my willpower.

"Baby, Love, Lord knows I want this more than anything, but I think we should wait."

"No, I need you now. Please?" she begs. Goddamnit, she fucking begs. She's going to be the death of me.

"Katie, are you sure?"

"Yes, now fuck me like you used to."

I pull a condom from my wallet, and grip it in my palm. Katie pries it from my hand and rolls it on me. Just that tiny task is about to make me combust. She then lifts her dress and slides down my dick, and wholly fucking hell.

"Good God, Katie. You feel so good," I grunt out.

She sits still to adjust to the intrusion because I'm thicker and longer than most, not to toot my own horn. She then begins to bounce on my dick like she's a fucking pro, and to be honest, now I know why she's such a fucking pro... fuck; the girl I can't live without has just about fucked every man known to mankind...shit.

And just like that, I can't erase that fucking thought out of my head.

Damnit!

I have to, or she'll know the moment I no longer get hard...but wait. I'm still as hard as a steel rod. As if that thought doesn't phase my manhood at all. This my pussy! Not anyone else's. Fuck those assholes! She's mine!

Goddamnit, she's mine...

And in that moment, I no longer have those thoughts again. Katie is mine, and she'll never be anyone else's.

I reach down to play with her clit, pressing firmly on her tiny bud, while she fucks the shit out of me, bouncing and moaning, and for a moment, I forget we're in the fucking park, fucking each other like horny dogs in heat.

"Ah, yes, Jackson. I've missed this. I've missed you."

"I've missed you too, Love." I wrap my arms around her waist and force her to let me take charge. I thrust my dick into her, filling her completely. She starts to moan loudly, so I stuff my handkerchief in her mouth to muffle her cries. I play with her clit, while I slam my dick up in her, over and over again, until I feel her slick walls clamp down on me, suffocating my dick, and in that moment I know she's about to come all over me. And if memory serves me right, she's a squirter, so I'll have to lift her up and let her come into my mouth, so we won't be a complete mess.

"Baby, you about to come?" I ask her.

"Uh huh," and just when she leans over me, I lift with all my strength, steady her over my mouth, wrap my lips around her pussy, and suck for dear life. Then, with every ounce of her being, she screams out, letting her juices squirt directly into my mouth, down my tongue, and into my throat, and my God, that was the best fucking juice I ever had.

My juices. Exquisitely sweet and sour taste, like sour patches...similar to her. Tangy at first, but once you break through her walls, she's as sweet as the taste of her juices.

"Oh, good God, Jackson!" she screams ecstatically. Panting and moaning, her release coming down slowly.

"I have to help you get yours." And before I can protest, she's climbing down my body like a fucking monkey, ripping the condom off my dick and taking me in her mouth, all of me, and I can only last seconds before I'm squirting into her mouth in pure carnal ecstasy, using my hands to muffle my own goddamn cries.

"Fuck, Katie!" She continues sucking beyond my sensitivity, and I nearly buck off the ground. I have to take her to my room. But she's not letting go, and she's doing what I've done to her, pleasuring me, with those fuckable lips of hers, until I gift her my cum once again, something I didn't think was even possible. And the sight of her taking me, drinking me, is driving me insane.

God, I'm nowhere close to being done with her.

I lift her up, and we both adjust our clothing. "Come with me, Katie. Come to my room," I demand, hoping to hell she says yes. That this, this what we have, isn't over. Not yet.

"Okay," and before she can change her mind, I take her hand into mine and damn near drag her down the sidewalk of the park and head straight for the mansion.

JUST LIKE OLD TIMES, WE FUCK, AND WE MAKE LOVE, AND then we fuck again until the sun spreads across our naked bodies through the bay window of my hotel room.

We hold each other, never letting go in fear we'll fall and never find our way again. Entangled in the sheets, I glide my calloused hands over her scarred skin. I wondered where she got them all this time, but I never wanted to put her on the spot. Instead, I wanted to allow her the opportunity to open up to me on her own time. And she is, slowly, but she is, and I couldn't be prouder.

"I got them that night," she confesses in such a small voice I don't even recognize it. "At the time, I felt the slicing of my skin, but it didn't register that they were cutting me, marking me, scaring my delicate skin. I never even felt the pain until I managed to make it to the ER that night. And to be honest, all of that is a blur, just a big blob of darkness," she releases as a prayed weight lifted off her shoulders.

"Do you remember anything else about that night?"

"Bits and pieces. More like a nightmare on repeat every time I close my eyes."

"I had no idea."

"How could you? I never revealed any of this."

"But if I noticed the discomfort, you had while sleeping, I could of—"

Cutting me off, "I just realized that I don't have them when I'm with you. It's only when I'm alone," she divulges. And it's like music to my ears. "Shoot, I have to head to my room and get dressed. I promised Harper I'll set everything up for their departure." And just like that, the moment is gone.

"Can I see you again?" I ask meekly, something I never do, but with her, I'm a different man. Not wanting to put too much pressure on her, but needing another night, another day, another moment with her. I'll take anything I can get at this point.

"Yes," she states firmly, confidently. "I would love that," thank the heavens above. Not all is lost.

CHAPTER NINE
KATHERINE

LIFE HAS BEEN BLOWN into my lungs, awakened to a brand-new day as if the past never existed. Jackson is everything I never expected. I knew he was a good person, but damn. He's compassionate, thoughtful, and boy, does he know how to suck pussy and fuck me thoroughly. He knows me well, catering to and comforting me when I need it most but not overbearing where I can't breathe or think. Our lovemaking was very different somehow. Like more feeling in every stroke; more passion and intimacy. Saying those words to me would have scared the living hell out of me in the past. And even though I'm not ready to share those intimate words, just yet. I can show him how much I care; how much I need him and above all, how much I want him.

I'm not going to lie; he pissed me the fuck off during the wedding, but boy, did he make up for it, and I love every minute of it. My skin still tingles with his touch, and makes me feel alive, wanted, needed, something I never felt from anyone else.

As I pack the last items of Harper's things and place them in the trunk of their SUV, I hear my name being called. But not my God-given name, my name from a different time.

"Clarity...Clarity Rose. Is that you, honey?" I don't move a muscle because if I alert this random person that I may be the person they are talking about, I'll never live it down. "Clarity! Hey, it is you. How have you been?"

The tiny hairs on the back of my neck stands, goosebumps flair as my breathing hitches a beat in my throat. Closing my eyes and taking a much-needed breath, I turn slowly to brace myself.

"Jazzy? Oh my gosh!" I gush with relief in my bones. "It's been so long," I say, glad it's her and not one of my old clients.

Jazzy Lisa was a young girl just like me, trying to find her place in this cruel world. During that time, she was using drugs heavily and always so paranoid and self-conscious. She wanted so much to please everyone, losing herself along the way.

"Yes, it has. Gurl, I had a kid, left that shit show, and am now married to an incredible man. He's changed my life completely," she spews with such love and affection. "We own a business together, and it's thriving."

"Wow, that's great to hear. I love learning that we can overcome our past."

"Yes! I go to church now and finally finish school like you always pestered me. It was you that encouraged me, told me I could be more than a stripper, showed me that I can be the person I want to be if I work hard for it."

Wow, I didn't know I made such an impact in someone's life. I don't know how much I can take before crying. This lump in my throat is about to burst.

"I'm so happy for you."

"Thank you! What about you? How's life treating you?"

"Well, I did finish school. I'm a cop now. Not married though and no kids...." I lie. But she doesn't have to know that part of my life. I want her to have something to look up to and know even through all of my trials and tribulations, I still made it through, barely.

"That's great! A cop. Who would have thought, but I'm proud of you; I'm proud of us. Look at us, all family savvy and shit."

"Yes, savvy and shit!"

"Well, I have to run. I have to take the kids to the dentist."

"Okay, nice seeing you again. By the way, what's your number? We can hang out sometime," I ask.

Jazzy sends me her number and then takes off running around Forsyth Park as I finish packing the trunk. Wow, little ole me making a difference in people's lives. Not just people, my fellow stripper family. I had no idea she was even listening to me.

I'M SITTING HOME ON MY PLUSHED SOFA, SIPPING ON A refreshing melon-flavored martini, affrighting myself; psyching myself out.

Panicking...

Losing my everlasting mind...

Basically losing my shit...

Using the alcoholic beverage to soothe my nerves...

Why did he have to say those words to me? Those three precious words that torments me ever chance they get. Those three exorbitant little words that formulates my own kind of hell.

I can't do this.

He can't love me. *I won't let him...*

I have to walk away, no slither in the night to get as far away from him at all costs.

But then, there's a voice in my head telling me to stop worrying; stop letting other people dictate my happiness or my understanding of the truth.

It's telling me to get in touch with myself instead. Focus on what makes me happy...but what what makes me smile, what brings joy into my life?

I don't have the answer to the questions I seek, but of course that voice is telling me to love who I am, love all of my flaws, my insecurities, my craziness, my awkwardness, my weirdness, my intensity, my vulnerabilities, my everything.

That cantor simply wants me to be myself.

I'm listening...

At least I'm trying to listen.

In order to ever move forward in my life, I have to accept my destiny.

I just have too...

IT'S MONDAY MORNING, AND I SERIOUSLY DID NOT FEEL LIKE coming to work. But I make it anyway.

I have to face Jackson since I basically ignored him all day yesterday. Not to hurt him by any means. Hell, I just got shit to figure out and I'm almost there, I just need him to get on the same page, uh, maybe the same wavelength... Hell, I don't have a clue at this point.

I just have to get out of my head and live the life I crave.

Let's just say...uh, well, I'm trying—seriously.

After roll call, Jackson and I head to Debi's for breakfast. Because of course we're partners and I can't avoid him forever. Besides, we're back on days, and I'm grateful for the change. A much needed change if you ask me.

On the ride to Debi's, I sense a change in the atmosphere, a shift in Jackson's and my interaction. The air is thick and charged but nowhere hostile.

This is promising—very promising.

"So, we have to make some rules while we're partners," I begin.

"Sure, rules. Wouldn't expect anything different from you," he states firmly, not in a condescending way, but I'm open to anything kind-a-way. Very refreshing. This thing between us might just work.

"Rule number one, no fucking while working."

"Damn. I guess that's out of the question," he jokes.

"Jackson, I'm serious."

"I'm serious too. You just ruined my entire day."

"Whatever," rolling my eyes. "Rule number two—"

"What can be more damning than rule number one?" he asks incredulously.

"Staring at me like you want to fuck me, touching me, groping me, making side comments about fucking me...."

"That sounds like four rules in one. Are you sure you can follow your own rules? I've seen how you be looking at me," he teases.

"Look, last year, I'm aware that we fucked like bunnies. But it's different now. Then, we were just fucking, and now, well, now we're dating," I explain.

"Ouch. Just fuck buddies. I thought we were way more than that," he states a little hurt, placing his palm over the area where his heart, like actual organ resides.

"Fuck, this isn't coming out right," I admit with frustration. But nevertheless, I'm trying to do the right thing.

"Katie, I know what you mean. A clean slate and a spik-n-span slate it'll be," he singsongs, and all my frustrations evaporate.

God, how did I get so lucky...how?

We pull up to the East Bay Inn, where Debi's is housed. It's old but chic, small but quaint, and I love the southern cooking they deliver in the hotel's basement. As you walk down the stairs, the interior is made of the Savannah brick everyone is so crazy for. Back then, the structures were built with heart and passion. Now, I'm afraid just a simple storm will knock over most of these new buildings while the old keep holding on.

The hostess greets us and shows us our table. "It'll be just two?"

"Yes ma'am," I answer.

"Right this way. By the way, thank you for your service. We just love the police and will always support y'all. So, thank you," she gushes as we take our seats.

"Why thank you, ma'am. You are certainly welcome, and we're glad to do what we do," Jackson explains in that southern accent I always loved. It doesn't always come out, but he definitely lays it on thick for the southern belle we call our hostess.

"My name is Mary Sue if y'all need anything," definitely a southern belle with that name. She walks off, and Jackson glances at me with those panty-dropping emeralds of his. He has this smirk that just knocks me out every time.

"What?" I ask self-consciously.

"I'm thrilled you gave us a second chance. I know it was difficult. I just wanted to say that."

"One step at a time."

Mary Sue returns to take our orders, and we chat a little before our food arrives. I love their fish and grits with brown gravy. It's so decadent. As we eat, we hear a call go out about another missing girl, and my thoughts flood with the images of that night again. Man, when will this end? I'm so tired of reliving that horrific night. Maybe Jackson is right. Perhaps I need to speak to someone.

"Twenty-seven bravo one and two, can y'all ride that call?" Dispatch asks.

Jackson responds, "Ten-four."

"Mary Sue, can we have to-go boxes? Duty calls," I explain.

"Sure, and your food has been paid for, so don't worry about a thing," she assures us.

"Oh, thank you, but you didn't have to do that."

"It wasn't me, but I'll certainly thank them for you when I see them again. They're regulars."

She brings us two boxes, and I fill them with our half eaten breakfast. Jackson leaves a fifty-dollar tip on the table, and we walk out. I love that about him. He's always thoughtful, even when he doesn't have to be.

When we get in the vehicle, Jackson reads off the call. "It sounds like the fourth friend is now missing from Saint Vincent School. The school called this time, so we should be headed that way."

WE ARRIVE MOMENTS LATER AND ARE APPROACHED BY THE Headmaster, Connie Lovenett. "Hi, I'm the Headmaster. Can we talk in my office?"

"Yes, ma'am," I respond. Jackson and I follow her into the school, down the hall, and into her luxurious office designed in pristine white furniture with black and white scenery photos on the walls.

"Serenity Bostick was taken from school about fifteen minutes ago."

"What do you mean taken," I question.

"One of my guards witnessed Serenity being taken from the school grounds. We have footage of it, and we've alerted her parents. They're on their way," she explains.

"This is an abduction. Not a missing person. We must call an alert, SVU, and a supervisor," Jackson barks.

"Yes, I know. Let me think a minute. Ma'am, can we see the video footage?" I need to see exactly what happened.

She rewinds the video on the large screen for us to see the events unfold. But something captures my attention— As the video plays, I see a young girl standing at the corner of the building reading a book. Almost like she's waiting on someone. But wait, it's like looking at myself in the mirror fifteen years ago. The footage is a little blurry, but I can't tear my eyes from the screen, pausing the video to get a better look. Her hair is cut short, with curly ringlets falling in her smooth dark face. Her skin is so shady and soft that it takes my breath away. Her eyes large, brown, and pure. Just like mine. And her lips...my God... her full lips can bring any man to his knees.

I see a tall person walk into view of the camera, the person has a hoodie on, probably to block their appearance from the surveillance cameras. She's talking to this person as if she knows them. But then he grabs her arm, and she pulls away, arguing with him. He then punches her in the face and knocks her unconscious, falling to the ground hard. The male then lifts her over his shoulder and carries her to a vehicle, half in the screenshot and half out. He then jogs around the car, starts it, and drives off.

I'm stunned, speechless, and the nightmares I've been having are replaying all over again. But this time, my nightmares are my reality.

It can't be… there's no way…

It's not her… but I have a strange feeling…it is her.

CHAPTER TEN

KATHERINE

THE ENTIRE DEPARTMENT is running around, searching every corner, every hole, and every rock for the four missing teenage girls.

Except for me, I'm held up in an interview room to be questioned by Sgt. Maui and her lieutenant.

Why, I'm not sure. But whatever. I'll sit, wait, and twiddle my thumbs to keep my mind off everything.

Yeah right. Who the hell am I kidding? There's no way I can keep my mind off this shit right now...

I watch the news on the TV, and on a loop, the story is played over and over again. "There are now four teenage girls missing from a local private school," the broadcaster flashes the girls' pics across the screen. One Black female, beautiful, dark, with mesmerizing brown eyes. She has short curly hair and skin so pure and flawless; you can eat right off her face. At the bottom of the screen, her name flashes across, Emma Bactive. Then there's a Hispanic girl looks relatively young if you take all the makeup off. Her hair is dyed in so many colors, but it looks fantastic on her, layered just right. Her name is

NICOLETTE JOHNSON

Maya Hernandez. The next photo is Vivian Blanchard. She's a White female, and she's charming as well. She has long peanut butter color hair, curly, draped around her face. Flawless, pale, yet with a hint of pink shades her skin. Her build is of muscular physique as if she plays sports. And the last photo stands out more than the rest. It's like looking at myself in the mirror fifteen years ago. I can't tear my eyes from the screen, pausing the live broadcast because we can certainly do that now. Her hair is cut short, with curly ringlets falling in her face with a head band taming the rest. Her dark skin is so smooth and unharmed or undamaged. Her eyes doppy, large, brown, and pure. Just like mine. And her lips...well... her full lips can tell a story of a thousand people. Her name is so suiting for her, Serenity Bostick, so pure and innocent. I keep replaying the scene over and over again.

When Jackson caught on to my reaction to the surveillance at the school, he had no choice but to step in. I was in no condition to continue my duties. I was frozen; stopped in a time capsule that kept replaying over and over again. I'm pretty sure he told my deepest secrets; I can't blame him, nor be mad at him. It's our job. My secrets could possibly help a person survive. Help those innocent girls who have brightened futures ahead of them. This is bigger than me, and I realize that now.

About an hour later, Sgt. Maui walks in with a clipboard in her hand and several folders. "Hi, Cpl. Harris, do you know why I have you here?"

"No, ma'am," I lie. I need her to explain to me what she knows in grave detail whether I want to hear it or not.

"Well, Cpl. Henry stated you had a child fifteen years ago and that one of the missing girls could be her. How am I doing so far?"

"I—I," taking a deep breath. You got this. You know who you are, and you know what you've overcome. This is just another setback. "You're correct. I did have a child, and I gave her up for adoption. But I have no idea if she's one of the missing girls," I state firmly because it's the truth. I don't really know.

"I see. Are you aware that Serenity Bostick is adopted?"

"No, ma'am. I left the scene prior to the reveal of that information," well to be honest, I completely shut down, my body refusing to move forward, so yeah. I missed that whole conversation whether it was had in front of me or not. I couldn't be sure even if I tried.

"Yes, she's adopted, and after seeing photos of her, she's definitely your twin; if not, your doppelgänger," she spits out.

"Why am I here?" Ignoring her statement.

"Because you may be able to help us find the missing girls."

"How so?"

"Do you know this person in the photo?" she slides a photo to me that depicts a large, tall, dark-skinned man sporting a goatee and bald head. His smile sickens me, with that gold tooth in the front flashing at me like it used to, taunting me. My skin crawls just thinking of the way he treated me and those girls years ago. My heart begins to race, pounding through my rib cage at the mere image of him.

"Yes, I know him. That's Bobby, Bobby Frazier. He's the manager of the strip club I used to work at years ago. I gave that life up a long time ago. So why are you bringing it up now?" I thought I did damn good covering up that part of my life…

But that damn video…

"Because we think this man is connected to the disappearance of those girls."

And just like that, that night come flashing before me, the slicing, the ripping, the tearing of my skin.

My breath hitches, and I can't breathe on my own anymore. My body spasming at a rate I didn't think possible.

Something is trapping my air; I can't breathe. I feel my throat closing, clotting. Something I felt years ago.

Panicking, I grasp for my chest, the stinging pricks of pain piercing my veins.

I hear Sgt. Maui in the distance calling my name and requesting EMS, but I can't respond.

I can't speak.

What's happening to me?

I don't know what to do.

Please, God, please help me.

Why can't I breathe?

I start to see dark spots and my skin is burning, the heat erupting throughout and I know it's only a matter of time before I pass the hell out, but I have to hold on. I try so hard to hold on for just another moment. *I have to hold on.*

This can't be my demise. It just can't be.

CHAPTER ELEVEN

JACKSON

AFTER HOURS of watching video surveillance, flock cameras, and tag readers, my phone ping with a message. It's from Sgt. Maui. Hours ago she said she wanted to speak with Katie based on the information I gave her. I know Katie will be mad, but I had no choice. If Serenity is her child, then Sgt. Maui must know the truth to find her, whether it's small or not.

Hopefully Sarge has an update for me.

Sgt. Maui: Meet me at the hospital. Your partner blacked out.

What?

What the actual fuck did I just read? Staring in disbelief. What happened? I search around, looking for someone to take me to the hospital. Katie has the vehicle with her. Perez is just up the street when I see him step out of his vehicle. I take off, running towards him.

"Hey Perez, can you drop me off at the hospital? There's something wrong with Katie."

"Sure, man. Hop in."

NICOLETTE JOHNSON

We jump in the car, and I'm praying to God she's okay. I knew this was a lot for her, but I had no idea she was under this much stress.

No idea.

We arrive moments later, and I wave Perez off and jog to the front door. "Hey, Sarge, what happened?"

"We were talking one moment, and the next, she was scratching at her throat as if she couldn't breathe; her eyes rolled back, and I knew something was wrong."

"What were y'all talking about, if you don't mind me asking."

"No, not at all. We were talking about her former boss, Bobby Frazier."

"Doesn't ring a bell, but Katie is very private about her life. So I don't know much."

"But she opened up about giving a kid up when she was a teenager?" Sgt. Maui questions skeptically.

"Yeah. She discloses just enough to settle your craving but not enough to curve your appetite. If you know what I mean?"

"Oh, I know. Just curious. That's all," surrendering to defeat.

The doctor approaches us as I turn to look out the window.

"Hi, I'm Dr. Calloway. Are y'all family?" he asks.

"No, she's my partner. Is she going to be okay?" I ask, not caring if I'm family or not. I'm the only family she got right now. Harper and Dom are out of the country for their honeymoon. I'm not disturbing them if I don't have to.

"Yeah. She'll be okay. Her blood pressure plummeted, and that's why she blacked out. I know your profession can be stressful, but she's under a tremendous amount. Is there any way she can take a leave of absence?" the doctor asks.

"She's not going to like that at all. You might as well ask her to cut her left leg off. She's a very determined, stubborn woman. Only you can make her stay home and do nothing," I suggest, staring at the doctor, because I refuse to get cursed out by Katherine Harris.

"Then, that's what I'll do. Because if she doesn't take it easy, she'll be having open heart surgery the next time I see her," Dr. Calloway explains the severity of her condition.

"Mission 'Take it Easy' coming right up," I agree, and he walks away.

"We both know she's not just going to sit and twiddle her thumbs while this case unravels," Sgt. Maui states.

"Yes, I know. But if I can sway her just a little, I might just get my way." All I need is a iron-tight plan.

"Isn't the Music Festival this week?" Sgt. Maui asks, and I know exactly where her mind is going.

"Yep. I'll see if I can get tickets to the Trustee's Garden to watch Cory Wong and KINFOLK. If memory serves me right, she loves funk and jazz music," I praise myself. "Thanks, Sarge."

"No, thank you. I need her in my unit. She's useless to me in the hospital."

"What do you mean?" I ask a little confused. Katie never mentioned joining SVU.

"She didn't tell you?" pausing at my confusion, "Okay, so, I asked her to join my unit, and she accepted."

"Oh, I didn't know," clearing my throat. I remind myself this is good news. "She will do great. She probably didn't say anything in fear that it won't happen. You know all too well how people make promises around here, knowing damn well they can't keep them."

"Oh, it's happening. Sooner than I thought." And she turns and walks away like the information didn't just change everything.

But I'm happy for Katie. She deserves to get everything she's worked hard for. She's such a compassionate and genuine person. Sgt. Maui couldn't have selected a better person for the position. She will absolutely thrive. And I pray I'll be by her side to witness it all.

CHAPTER TWELVE
KATHERINE

GOSH DARNIT! I'm so embarrassed! Ugh, I just want to crawl up in a corner and die. I can't believe I passed out in the interrogation room like; who does that? I'm totally innocent in all of this shit, and I'm the one who passes the hell out!

From what the doctor explained, whether I believe it or not, my body is under a tremendous amount of stress and it will shut down whether I like it or not. So, to slow me completely down, he has placed me on mandatory leave because he didn't have faith that I'd take the leave on my own. Hell, he's probably right about that.

I have four teenage girls I need find… but first, let me wallow in self-pity… cause, why the hell not…

Balled up in the fetal position on my queen-size bed, I listen to Marian Hill's Deep, which quickly gets me in a mellow mood. Then, using the remote, I turn it up to the highest tempo, feeling the beat vibrate through me.

I don't care if I disturb the neighbors. I don't care if I blow my eardrums. I don't care about anything right now.

But for some reason my body's betraying me like no other. Listening to this song, trying to make me do things my mind don't want to do. But, here we are listening to this f-ing song. This song right here gets me out my bed, stretching my legs, and dancing my worries away, dancing my fears away, dancing my frustrations away.

This song knows me so well because I'm in so deep, always in my head and words. I just want to let it all go…I have too.

I put my phone on Do Not Disturb just to get relief for a moment. Then, of course, the song switches to the badest of them all, Listening…

I know exactly what I need…

Picking up my phone and sending a text to the person I need the most right now.

Me: I NEED YOU!

Moments later…

Jackson: I'm on my way!

No questions asked.

Thank the heavens, and with that, 'Don't Let Go' plays next, and it arises something in me…I want him; I need him. So, the moment he knocks on my door, I yank him in, snatch off his clothes, and ride him for dear life.

No condom, no protection, no nothing. Just him and me and I don't care anymore.

And he doesn't stop me…

Sweating, panting, and grunting our pleasure.

His dick thrust inside me, shattering every negative thought I ever had, if only for a moment, and when 'I'm Still in Love with You,' by New

Edition comes on, we're no longer fucking. Instead, we're making sweet, sweet love to each other.

His hands caressing me firmly but gently. His kisses spreading across my skin like a prayer, and every stroke of his pleasure awakens something new inside me. The passion alone is so overwhelming I can't stop the tears threatening to break free.

"Oh, God," I cry out through each panting moan as he takes one of my nipples into him warm soft mouth, sucking fiercely and my God I see stars bursting, digging my nails into his stiff muscles. Hearing him groan in pleasure is music to my ears.

And when 'Under the Influence,' by Chris Brown, cycles through the atmosphere, I know we belong to each other because nothing else than this speaks volumes to me; to us.

Jackson makes sweet, sweet love to me repeatedly, and I give all of me to him with an open heart.

His mouth on my pussy, licking gently and so lightly, teasing me to oblivion. Finally, I can't take it anymore, bucking off the floor, forcing his tongue to enter me firmly and swiftly.

He presses my arms to my side, forcing me to take his torturous endeavor.

"Please, Jackson!"

"Please what, Love."

"I need more," I beg.

"No, Love. I'm taking control. I'll pleasure you how I want, and you'll just lay there and take it. Understand?"

And when I don't answer, he slaps my pussy with his hand, and twist one of my nipples firmly and I nearly flip him off me. But not him. He's way too strong for me to toss in this state. My body is like Jell-O, like mush underneath him, and I can only do one thing; comply with his commands. Something so hard for me to do; let someone else take control.

"Yes, I understand," giving in entirely to his commands.

He makes love to my pussy with his mouth so hungrily, so greedily. I feel myself build up, yet again, and I know it's only a matter of time before I lose complete control and the moment he nips on my tender spot, I come so hard, I squirt into his mouth, and he drinks from me like he's been starving for this very moment and it turns me completely on, I thrust for more and more.

I'm such a needy, horny freak right now. But I don't care. I need to feel him inside of me again and again.

"Jackson, oh God Jackson, I love you," I whisper softly in his ear, finally able to relay the same sentiment I know he yearns for.

"I love you too, Love," and with that, Jackson gives me multiple orgasms over and over again and him filling me completely with his cum, satisfying me beyond belief.

We lay together in each other's embrace on the floor, perfectly content with each other's company. His fingers feathering my skin, causing me to relax and drift into a blissful state of mind. And we both fall asleep to 'Something in My Heart,' by Michel'le, playing on the surround sound music bar.

Perfectly content.

I AWAKE IN MY BED, WITH MY THROW BLANKET OVER MY BODY. I must have been out cold because I never even felt or even realized I was taken to bed after our lovemaking.

I sit up and stretch. I notice I have a sundress at the foot of the bed. I also hear commotion in the kitchen.

Snickering a little because I'm such a giddy mess. I don't think I've ever experienced anything remotely to the feeling I feel right now.

I jump out of the bed, throw on my Kimono, and rush to the kitchen to find out what he got up his sleeves.

"Hey, beautiful! Did you get some rest?"

"Much needed rest! Thank you. Whatcha cooking?"

"Making you a seafood omelet. Here's your mimosa, peach with a splash of lavender."

"Wow, I've never known you to cook."

"You never gave me a chance to cook for you."

"Okay, you're right. I'm learning to let people in."

"And you're doing a fine job at it. Now sit and let me pamper you. Besides, the doctor said you need to get some rest."

"And three hours of making love is taking it easy?" I question sarcastically.

"Well, you didn't give me much choice when you jumped me the moment I crossed your threshold."

"Whatever. You know you wanted it as much as I needed it."

"Touché."

"So, where are we headed? I see you pulled out a sundress for me."

"To the Music Festival in the Trustee's Garden."

"Ooh, live music. I love live bands."

"Yes, I know. But first, I gotta feed you, keep you hydrated because I'm making love to you one more time before we go."

And at that command, I'm already soaking my panties from the desire creeping to my core.

NICOLETTE JOHNSON

Damn!

After we eat, he makes good on his promise, captivating my entire being. This man has made me feel more alive than I've ever felt before.

But I know what he's doing. He's trying to take my mind off those missing girls, and for now, I'll oblige his temptation. Besides, I needed to be thoroughly fucked and pampered, if you must know.

THE OPEN SKIES ARE CLEAR, WITH THE SUN KISSING MY melatonin skin, giving it a dubious shine. Jackson just parked his silver Chevy Tahoe along the street, allowing me to step onto the curb, out of harm's way. We then grab our blankets, lounge chairs, and pillows from the trunk area.

It couldn't have been a better day, even if I had the capability to influence the weatherman himself. As we walk towards the venue, Jackson takes my hand into his, which catches me off guard because I never had such tenderness directed towards me. Never.

He guides me through the gates, where security checks our bags and tickets.

"Here are your bands. You'll be seated in the VIP section," the hostess explains as she places our bands on our wrists. "Oh, and here are your beverage tickets. You can redeem them at the bar. Enjoy the show," giving us a warm smile as we walk through the gates.

There's funk music drifting around us, and the atmosphere is so laid back that it takes me aback. It's been a while since I've been to a live band concert, and to be able to picnic too that's a plus in my book.

Jackson guides me to the VIP section, where we find an area secluded from everyone else; so we can watch the band play and have some alone time. We help each other with the spread of the blankets and the placement of our chairs and pillows.

"What would you like to drink," Jackson asks as I place the last pillow on the blanket. It's charming to be cared for. I feel like a giddy princess in a Disney movie. Even last time was unbelievably romantic every time I was with Jackson. He makes me feel so wanted and loved in everything he does. He always put me first.

Always.

"I'll take whatever IPA they offer."

"A girl after my own heart. Coming right up." He then swiftly leaves, allowing me to lie and listen to some nice funk and jazz music.

As I close my eyes. I get this strange feeling as if someone's watching me, so I shift to see who it is. Not seeing anyone, I close my eyes back. Moments later, I feel my hair stand on my skin, and I know there's something up. So, I sit up and scan the area.

Just beyond the iron gates, I see someone standing across the street near the Eastern Wharf. It's the new area that's being built for the ridiculously wealthy because, let's face it, none of us common folk can afford to even walk down their street.

I can't tell if it's a guy or a girl standing there or if they are even gawking at me or just enjoying the music without paying, but I seem to get a terrible feeling that something or someone watching me, and usually, when I get that feeling, it's right.

"Hey Love, here's your beer, and they were selling gator bites at the food truck, so I got us some with fries," Jackson announces as he hands me my beer and sits in the lounge chair.

I look over my shoulder, and the unidentified person holding up the corner is no longer there, but I keep my alertness slightly above normal just in case.

"Thanks, Jackson."

"For what?"

"Doing this. Taking my mind off things. I know I need to take it easy, but I can't stop thinking about those girls."

"I know, but just for a day, I'd like you to focus on something else, like relaxation."

After a moment of contemplating his request, I reply, "Okay, if only for a day." And that's all it takes before he's leaning over me and taking my lips into his with such purpose and passion I forget we're surrounded by people before he ends the kiss with a loud smack and me falling forward in need of more connection, more, more everything from this gift of a specimen.

"Tonight. Wait until tonight… I'm not finished with you yet."

CHAPTER THIRTEEN
JACKSON

IT TOOK SOME CONVINCING, but I finally got Katie to pack a bag and stay with me until her medical leave was done. She's such a stubborn woman, but she knows more than me; she needs to take it easy. High blood pressure is nothing to play with. It's a silent killer among women, especially for her age. With the stress of our profession and the hand she was dealt since birth, she has to learn to channel her frustrations and stress agitators with something healthier.

And using me as her personal stress reliever, her personal sex toy is all kinds of blissfulness I'm willing to give every night and day. We've fucked, made love, and fucked some more, and I'll be damned to stop it now. I've waited, no, I've yearned for her all year, and now that I have my sex fanatic back, I'll be damned to let her go. I can do this every day until my dick falls off, and even then, I'll fuck her with my tongue, fingers, toes, you name it, and force her orgasms right out of her soul.

I love this woman more than I cared to admit before, but now that I know she loves me back, it'll take God himself to rip her from me.

It's been a few days, and we are no closer to finding the young teenage girls. And I know it's driving Katie crazy, but I must keep her mind off what's happening. What better way to do that than making sweet, sweet love to my one and only... again and again and again.

I haven't allowed her to leave the bed because worshiping her body comes easy to me in every way. Tenderly kissing each scar as if they're my own to pleasure, caressing every delicate part of her skin, making her moan my name, gives me ammunition to pursue her needs completely. A flick of my tongue or a feathering of my fingers across her sensitive parts awaken something in me and her. Wanting to bring her to the brink of no return forces me to devote all of me into her. And only when she beckons me to continue, only then will I passionately fill every infatuation I have for her and me.

As I slide my fingers into her sweet pussy, she clinches around me, never wanting me to stop thrusting into her deeper. She's so incredibly hot right now, I massage my own dick in fear that I might just implode my damn self.

"Jackson, please?" She begs once again and of course I make her wait until I'm completely satisfied with my assignment. I want her completely sated, quenched before I enter her.

"Yes, Love..."

"I—I," she responds incoherently. And now, I know I've got her completely in my control.

I make my way up her body, feathering kissing in my wake, while my fingers make sweet love to her. I then replace my fingers with my dick, filling her, arousing her, stimulating her.

Katie wraps her legs around my waist, forcing me to tantalize her over and over again. I feel every curve of her sweet pussy, warm and slick.

"Jesus," is all I can manage to say, trying my damnedst to hold on for dear life. She feels so good right now, I can't get enough. I won't ever satisfy my cravings for her.

I thrust into her over and over again, curving and swerving my hips to meet her thrusts and I can no longer hold on, spilling my seed into her sweet and tender pussy.

No longer capable of holding my own body, I collapse next to her and fall the hell to sleep.

And now, I wonder, did I take her mind off the missing girls or did her pussy or maybe my dick. Who the hell knows, because right now, I don't give a damn what's happening outside this bedroom... not right now anyways...

IT'S MY GOAL TO MAKE KATIE FEEL AT HER UPMOST SELF, therefore, we decided to head downtown to enjoy a couple a drinks and a bite to eat while listening to some wonderful African tunes.

I've finished dressing when I hear Katie making her way downstairs. She enters the kitchen and my God, she's literally taking my breath away. Her hair styled in a way that I love, with small curls kissing her face. She's wearing a long flowing white dress, with several colorful flowers scattering about at the seam. The straps are hanging just right and what brings it completely together, are the pink chucks she's sporting. I can eat her right up.

"Ready?"

"Uh, yes of course. You look—amazing," I answer.

"Thank you. So do you, handsome," she kisses me on my cheek. "Love the blazer and jeans. It's so you."

I guide her out of the house into my truck, where I for the first time in my life, open the door for her. I know she can open the door herself, but I want her to feel cherished, loved, and like a princess if only for a night.

"So, where are we headed?" Katie asks.

"The new Baobab Lounge downtown."

"Yes, I've wanted to try that place. I can't wait. Everyone's been raving over it."

"Well, I'm glad I can oblige your many desires."

"Food and drinks, what else can a girl ask for?"

"Oh, I can think of a few things."

"I'm sure you can," she teases me.

About twenty minutes later, we parking in the public parking garage at the JW and make our way to the lounge. Upon entry we're swarmed with raw elements and modern elegance that comes to life with zebras, lions, giraffes, and so much more. Baobab is one of Savannah's best bars in the growing entertainment district. We're taken on an adventure and celebration of African cultures, enjoying the artwork from different regions of Africa. Then add the simplicity of custom cocktails and small delectable dishes that take your palate to a whole new level, and we're certain to be awaken to something beyond our beliefs.

The atmosphere, music and by God, the company of Katie is nothing short of an experience I'll never forget.

"This place is amazing. Thank you so much for bringing me here," Katie gushes.

"Anything for you, Love."

As we place our orders, Sophia enters with a guy we're not familiar with.

"Hey, is that Sophia?" I ask Katie.

As she glances over her shoulder, I notice Sophia tense up like we're the last people in the world she wanted to run into. Katie waves her over and she reluctantly obliges her request. I wonder if Katie notices or is she oblivious to Sophia's behavior, her uneasiness.

"Hey Sophia, would y'all like to join us? We have plenty of room and we just ordered, so you're right on time. I hear the food is spectacular," Katie continues to ramble.

"Um, yes," Sophia clears her throat. "I've been here before," Sophia admits.

The guy standing next to Sophia clears his throat after a moment of awkwardness.

"Oh, sorry. Katie, Jackson. This is Derrick Fields. Derrick, these are my friends and co-workers."

"Hey, it's nice to meet you," I extend my hand.

"Nice to meet y'all too," Derrick responds.

"So, what brings you two here?" Katie asks Sophia as she and Derrick take their seats.

"Well, Derrick is helping me with something," Sophia answers.

"Mysterious," Katie gushes.

"You'll find out in due time," Sophia promises.

Once our drinks and food arrive, the tension between us soothe out and in the next moment, we're laughing and joking around. Something that probably should have started to begin with. But neither here nor there.

Katie and Sophia head to the restroom, leaving Derrick with me and at first, he's mute silence, but then, I can't get him to shut up.

Asking questions like, do I watch football, or do I hang out a lot, and then there's him telling me who he is and where he's from and he'd like for me to join him at that sports club on Victory Drive. What's it called again?

Coach's Corner...that's right. It's house next to Eastside Precinct.

He's a weird dude and I don't know if he's nervous as all get out or he's as frugal as they come with his life story. Can't really put a finger on it, but I am damn glad to see Katie and Sophia exit the restroom and head back our way.

This is the oddest interaction I've ever been a part of.

"Jackson, come with me. I want to show you something," as she pulls on my hand toward a walkthrough in the lounge.

"Okay, okay. You're very giddy tonight. I've never witnessed this side of you."

"Well, I've decided to turn a new leaf. You're right. I need to loosen up a little and relax," she admits as she pulls me towards her leaning against the brick pillared walkway. "And, I know you've been trying to take my mind off the missing girls and although I don't think that's possible, I haven't allowed the thought of them to overshadow your love for me. And I wanted to thank you."

"Oh really," feathering my fingers over her exposed delicate skin. I have to admit, I love this side of her, but I also love the feistiness and sassiness. I love all of her.

And with that confession, I gift her with a kiss she'll never forget and a hardened manhood she'll never deny even if she tried.

The chemistry between us is combustible and it makes me want to live the rest of my days a happy man.

"Let's get out of here," I manage to whisper in her ear as I tear my lips from hers.

"I thought you'd never ask."

After paying the tab, we head to the house and we can't make one step into the house without ripping each other's clothes off.

Her dress, in shreds in a heap on the floor; my jeans and blazer strewn about the floor next to her panties and bra.

Her nipples taunt and needy, her skin velvety and pure. Lifting her for my own pleasure.

Katie wrapping her legs around my waist begging to be taken.

I take one throbbing nipple in my mouth while I tease the other with my fingers, grabbing and pulling like she like.

"Ah, Jackson," she signs in great pleasure.

I'm like a kid in a candy store, not knowing what I want more.

I carry her up the stairs into my bedroom and guide her across the bed, but not before I take her sweet, harden bud between my lips and thrust my fingers into her, curving them to gain complete control of her ecstasy.

And when she incapable of forming coherent words, I know then that she's mine and ready.

And there's nothing more than this moment right here, being the one that can satisfy my girl more than anything else…being everything to her, for her.

ONCE I RETURN TO WORK, MY MAIN MISSION IN LIFE RIGHT now is finding those girls. I've been helping SVU as much as possible, in between calls and on my days off, but every lead we have turns into a dead end. And something tells me that we'll need Katie's help moving forward, but how can I subject her to more stress, more anxiety, and more tension? I can't, and I won't, if I have anything to do about it.

I'm leaving work today, knowing Katie will have questions and knowing I don't have the answers she's seeking. And it breaks me a little more each day not being able to deliver what she wants, what she needs.

NICOLETTE JOHNSON

My phone rings, and of course, it's my mom. I've skipped our weekly Friday dinners, not wanting to face her torment anymore. I know she means well, but I also know the woman I'm in love with is not the woman she'd want me to be with, and instead of putting myself or Katie through that, I've just ignored her calls until now.

"Hey, Mom."

"That's all you have to say to me? Hey Mom," my mom spits out with irritation the moment I answer the phone. And...here we go.

"I've been busy at work, Mom."

"Too busy to call your mother back?" No, I just don't want to deal with your shit.

"No, you're right. What can I do for you."

"Well, for starters, you can join us for dinner, and I'm not taking no for an answer."

"Fine. I'll be there. And I'm bringing someone with me," not asking, but telling her...

"Really," I hear the annoyance turn into hopefulness.

"Yes, Mom, and I want you to treat her with respect."

"Are you serious? Why the hell would I disrespect any of my guests?"

"I don't know, Mom. You have a way of making people feel beneath you."

"I do not, and I'm appalled you'd even suggest such a thing. Who in the hell do you think I am?" she fires back. I don't think I ever heard my mom curse before. Damn. I can hear the displeasure in every syllable.

"Sorry, Mom. I'm just under a lot of stress with work. I didn't mean to offend you."

"Whatever. Dinner is at seven sharp. You and your date don't be late." And with that, she hangs up before I can even respond. Fuck!

Yep! She's pissed.

"Hey love, we've been invited to a dinner tonight. Are you up for it?" I express over the Bluetooth in my truck.

"Uh, sure. I'll just put the steaks in the fridge."

"Oh, no. You made dinner already."

"Nope, no, not yet. I was about to. I wanted it to be hot when you got home. No worries at all."

"Okay, good. I'll be home in a few."

"Where are we having dinner?"

"At my parents."

"Oh, uh, okay," she says, a little panicked.

"My parents will love you. Don't worry at all," I lie to her, hoping it's not a complete lie and maybe only a little white lie. I know my dad will like her anyways, and my sisters will definitely support me. Mom on the other hand...is questionable.

"Not worried...I just—I never did the 'meet the parents' thing."

"You'll do great, and if you're uncomfortable, we'll just leave. No worries at all. Besides, you'll get to meet my parents and my sisters, well, two of my sisters. My oldest sister lives in Atlanta and rarely visits."

"Okay. I'll be ready when you get here."

"Bet, see you soon, Love."

I pray to the heavens above as I disconnect the phone; I hope I'm not making a huge mistake.

CHAPTER FOURTEEN
KATHERINE

WE ARRIVE at Jackson's parent's house, and oh my God. This isn't a house; it's not even a home. It's a mansion, sitting in the middle of the Landings, a neighborhood that is definitely secluded from the rest of Savannah. Standing four stories high, with ten single-car garages, and a perfectly manicured lawn that goes on for miles into a river behind the home, you'd think it's a home from straight out of the movies. Or a museum staged for the very poor to hope and gawk at the life they'll never live.

I definitely don't belong here...

Fidgeting with my fingers because I'm freaking the hell out. Jackson must notice my uneasiness because he takes my hand into his and soothes the tension right out of my bones. God, he knows just how to calm me the hell down.

I just hope I don't make a fool out of myself.

Jackson turns to me and stares into my eyes with those gorgeous green irises, and I know without a doubt he won't let me fail. "Love, baby. Everything will be okay. I know my family will love you." He then kisses me on my forehead, and takes my frustrations away with just a simple peck to my skin. Soft and purposeful, bringing life to my chattery heart. He then places a soft kiss on my lips and the warmth and softness brings life into me. They part slightly, allowing my tongue to slip inside. He maneuver his tongue is such a way, I no longer have control of this moment. Swirling desire in my core, my goodness I can't get enough of just the mere fact of him choosing me and kissing me.

After several moments, he pulls away when he hears giggling behind us.

"Hey, brother. Now, I never thought I'd ever see the day you bringing someone home, let alone kissing her in the front yard of mother dearest manor," a slender yet curvy young woman states as she approaches. She has the same green piercing eyes and dirty blonde hair as Jackson, and I know without a doubt this must be one of his siblings.

"Katie, this is Jade, my baby sister, and her husband, William."

"Hi, it's nice to meet you both," I greet them.

"The pleasure is all ours. It's good to meet the woman who's occupied all of my brother's time and the woman who's responsible for leaving me to endure these dreadful dinners," Jade states sarcastically. Panic seeping in the pit of my stomach. What's with these dinners...

"Oh, I didn't—"

"Love, no need to apologize. My sister lives for these dinners," Jackson interjects.

"That she does," William states proudly. "It's very nice to meet you," extending his hand to shake mine. And I offer without hesitation. Something unusual for me, to say the least.

"So, are we going in or chillin' outside for the rest of the night? I'm totally down for the latter," another female state as she approaches us. She is also gorgeous with the same green eyes and dark blonde hair, but she's slightly taller and more thicker than Jade.

The resemblance in them all is remarkable.

"And Katie, this is my other sister, Jillian," Jackson introduces. "Where's what's his name?"

Ignoring his question, Jillian takes my hand into hers. I can't help staring because she looks so familiar. "Hi, I'm sorry. I don't mean to stare rudely, but do I know you from somewhere?" I ask, genuinely curious.

"You might. She's one of the Assistant District Attorneys," Jackson explains.

"Right, I believe I've worked some cases with you," I express.

"Oh, that's wonderful. Are you an officer too?" Jillian asks.

"Yes. Jackson and I are partners."

"Brother, tisk, tisk, tisk... You never told us you were seeing someone," Jillian chastises Jackson.

"Oh, it's my fault. I'm a very private person. Jackson here has changed me in more ways than one," compelling me to open up a little more each day.

"That's Jackie for you. A true romantic at heart," Jade gushes.

I'm definitely beginning to understand why he's so good with me and being patient. He's learned from the best.

"Shall we?" Jackson offers. "And don't think I didn't notice you avoiding my question," Jackson chastise Jillian.

"Oh, I didn't know I answered to you, Jackie," Jillian fires back, patting him on the cheek.

"We shall," Jade sings over Jackson and Jillian's bickering. And with that, we all stagger forward through the grand double doors held open by, what I assume is, the help.

JACKSON GUIDES ME INTO THE ESTATE, AND MY BREATH IS literally taken away. The palace's grand entrance, with a huge chandelier and large floor-length paintings on the wall, each telling a different romantic story than the next. The pale colors throughout the foyer bring a sense of serenity to the room.

That word, serenity, brings me back to the missing girls, but I shake it away for just tonight. Tonight is about winning the hearts of Jackson's family. And hopefully not make a complete ass out of myself.

There's a bar set up near the entrance of the main room. But why would I expect anything less?

Jackson offers to get me a drink while I take in my surroundings. I knew Jackson was from money, but I had no idea it was to this magnitude. What the hell is he doing being a cop. He should be a lawyer or doctor or something else other than a cop. Geesh...

Hell, why is he with *me*...

"Here, Love, I got you a blackberry lemon drop martini. I hope that's okay?"

"Yes, of course. Thank you." As I take a sip of my drink, which by the way, is way better than I make them, I hear an announcement that dinner is ready. As Jackson guides me to the dining room, an older couple glides down the staircase like two models from a magazine.

They are radiantly flawless; damn, now I feel uncomfortable with the simple dress I chose to wear. The woman, with dark blonde hair and a streak of grey on the sides of her temples, is the spitting image of Jackson's sisters. She's flat-out stunning, with a floor-length satin gown that hugs her curves with pure seduction. The man is too clean, straight to the bowtie he's wearing, with a beard and short salt and pepper hair styled to the side. If I had doubts about how Jackson would look when he got older, I certainly don't have them now. This man is every woman's wet dream and then some, especially in his heather grey suit.

I don't mean to gawk, but my goodness...

I sure as hell don't belong here.

The older couple greets each of Jackson's siblings before approaching Jackson and me. His dad embraces me quickly with a tenderly hug and really seems to be glad I'm here, but his mom, she's a different story. She's very cold and standoffish. Almost like she doesn't even want to breathe the same air as me. She does some kind of French kissing on each side of my face but dares not touch me in the process. It was so quick I didn't have the chance to acknowledge what she was doing. So, I just stand here, ridiculously.

She hugs Jackson and whispers something in his ear, but it's too muffled to register it.

Everyone else stands with a look of surprise on their faces, like they were expecting something more from this exchange.

We then enter the dining room without another word. Jackson's demeanor changes completely, and it seems that he doesn't even want to be here anymore.

I feel so alone right now, even though I'm surrounded by people; I just want to fall into the very hole they probably dug for me in the backyard.

We hear the doorbell and everyone looks to Jackson's mother inquisitively.

"Ah, yes. That must be Claudia. I forgot I invited her some time ago," Ms. Henry states mostly to Jackson than anyone else.

I feel the atmosphere shift and my lord, the tension could slice straight through all of us.

"Mom, are you serious right now?" Jade spits out first.

"What? I forgot we were having guest and it'll be incredibly rude to send her away now," Ms. Henry states firmly.

Moments later a young jaw dropping, lips hanging, woman strolls into the dining room. Her hair is very staggering with long curl-lets flowing around her round strikingly beautiful face. Her complexion is of creamy caramel, dipped in white glaze. She's tall with the shortest pleated dress I've ever seen at a function like this. She stands in heels, four inches in length, giving her a runway vibe. She's fucking way out of my league if she was brought here to take Jackson right from under my nose.

As she sits, all eyes are scanning between me and her and occasionally Jackson. I don't know if it's pity or scorn, or hate, or just simply outrage, but I definitely don't want to be here now.

Silence thickens and it's getting incredibly difficult to breathe.

Jackson's father breaks the ice first. "So, Jackson. How did you two meet?" thank goodness. An easy question.

"We worked on the same shift together for about two years and then became partners recently," Jackson explains, leaving a whole lot out.

"Really, that means you're an officer too, uh—"

"Katie, my name is Kathrine Harris. But everyone calls me Katie. And yes, Mr. Henry, that's correct."

"That's wonderful. Such an honorable profession," his dad states proudly. "And call me Jack."

"Thank you, Mr. Jack," I respond kindly.

"And what about your family? Do they live here," Mr. Jack asks. And there goes the easy questions.

"Um, well, my mom died when I was five, and my father, well—he's in prison for killing my mom," I state matter-factly, and I feel Jackson grab my hand underneath the table.

"I'm so sorry to hear that," Jillian offers.

"Oh, it was a long time ago," I explain.

"Still, it must be terribly hard to grow up without a mother and father," Jade states heartfeltly.

"Yes, but I've since learned how to cope with the loss."

"No child should have to live without parents. What has the world come to?" Mr. Jack asks rhetorically.

Ms. Henry begins, changing the subject, "Jackson, weren't you and Claudia hanging out for a while there?" his Mom asks out of nowhere.

And at that moment, it's the pivotal timestamp that changes everything; the dynamic of this family unfolds in this very trice.

"You just couldn't do it, hun Mom. You just had to ruin a moment for me to introduce a fiercely extraordinary woman to my family. You couldn't last one fucking hour without disgracing yourself and this family," Jackson spits out. "And to think, we haven't even been served our fucking dinner yet."

"Jackson, baby. It's okay," I try soothing him. He just threw me for a loop with that response. I've never witnessed him speak to anyone like this, especially his mom.

"No, it's not. This is what the fuck I was talking about, Mom, earlier. Remember, earlier, our conversation," and Jackson stands when she doesn't speak, pushing his chair over, causing everyone to jump at the loud crash. "Fuck this shit. Dad, Jade, Jillian, William, Love, Claudia, sorry, but I'm not doing this anymore. We sit around this fucking table pretending to be a happy fucking family, and for what? Mom, I don't want no White girl, I don't want Claudia; I don't want a rich preppy debutante; never have and never will. Katie is the woman for me. She makes me want more in life, livens me up, giving me a reason to thrive. She is more woman than any other broad you've tried your damndest to hook me up with. I'm sick of it, and I finally have had enough."

Jackson's mom finally speaks, and the words that come out of her mouth next floors me speechless. "You know better than to bring a Black nappy-headed hood rat into my home. You should have told me earlier that this is what you were bringing home," pointing to me. "I would have told you right then and there, don't you ever bring a filthy mutt into my home. Calling her Love—" And before I know it, I've thrown my cocktail in her face. And she stares at me with utter disgust.

The blue-colored martini sliding down her perfectly manicured outfit, staining each crease in its wake.

"Fuck you!" I seethe through clenched teeth. "I won't give you the satisfaction of completing that statement," I spit out, grabbing my bag and walking the fuck out of there, not even knowing if Jackson is behind me or not. I see red, and before I lose my shit, I have to get the fuck out of this house.

"Katie, Love. Please slow down," Jackson hot on my heels. "I'm so sorry that happened," Jackson explained.

"Let me ask one question," spinning around, catching him off guard with my abrupt halt.

"Anything."

"Did you know your mom would humiliate me like that?"

"Uh—" And I know my answer when he can't come up with simple words.

"Seriously, Jackson? How could you do that to me? How? And that fucking girl. What was that? Something to prove that I'm a simple hood rat that has no place in a fucking death trap such as this," I bellow from within pointing at that haunted house they call a home. I'm so... I'm so... "Aurgh," I scream in pure red-hot frustration.

"Look, I didn't know she would say something like that, but I do know that my mom is against inner-racial relationships. I just never thought she would be this rude in a million years. Never. I didn't know she was going to invite Claudia. I promise you." And when I don't respond, he begs. "Katie, please look at me. I need to know that we're okay. I promise you I'm nothing like that. I don't share the same values as my mom."

Tears running down my face, "Jackson, I could never take you away from your family. I know how it feels to not have a family, but I won't take that blatant disrespect from no one. I'm sorry this happened like this, but I'm not sure about any of this. And Claudia? Do you want to be with her? Is that the type of woman you're looking for?" shaking my head, thoroughly confused, frustrated.

"No, I've never dated her, nor do I desire to be with her. You're the one I want. You shouldn't be sorry. I don't think you were wrong. My mom was wrong," he tries to convince me.

"Jackie, Jackie," I hear one of Jackson's sisters calling after him. And that gives me the chance to wipe the tears from my cheeks.

"Fuck! I'm sorry. I really didn't mean for any of this to happen," he apologizes again.

"Katie, we're so sorry for our mom's behavior. We do not share the same sentiment, and I promise you we will never make you feel unwelcome like that again," Jade explains as Jillian approaches behind her.

"Yeah, Katie. We're so sorry. Here, let's go have drinks and get the hell out of here. What do you say?" Jillian suggests.

I stand there torn between getting the hell out of dodge and accepting this shit show for what it is.

"Please, Katie. We want to make it up to you," Jade implores.

"There is no making this shit up. I've dealt with people like that my whole life. Thinking they're better than me because I'm Black or growing up in foster care. I'm sick of it and won't stand for it anymore. Not from her, not from anyone."

"And you shouldn't," Jackson agrees.

I can see the pleading eyes of all three of them, and it's like looking into the souls of triplets. Their kind gazes piercing through me, making me believe that they aren't like their mom, and they genuinely want to get to know me, for me.

"Okay, fine. We can have drinks, but downtown. Nowhere near this place. No offense."

"None taken," Jackson utters.

"Yay!" They all sing together.

"Let me get my husband and purse. We'll meet y'all at the Grove."

"Wait, what about Claudia?" I question them.

"What about her?" They respond in unison.

"Answer received, loud and clear."

"Perfect! See you soon!" Jillian shouts as she follows her sister into the house.

"Thank you, Katie," Jackson sighs.

"Don't thank me. Thank your sisters. If it weren't for them, I'd call an Uber to get me right now. I can't believe you put me through that shit show."

"I'm truly sorry. I really thought my mom would behave herself."

"I know, and that's what pisses me off the most. Your mom couldn't even make it through drinks before she treated me like the help, and for that, I'm sorry you've had to endure that your whole life."

He then wraps his arms around me, allowing me to cry it out on his shoulder before placing me in the Tahoe and taking me downtown with his sister, Jillian, in the backseat.

CHAPTER FIFTEEN

JACKSON

NOT IN A MILLION years would I have guessed that my mom, Bethany Henry, would act in such a hastily manner. What the fuck was she thinking? I can't phantom ever treating anyone like that, let alone my child's girlfriend or boyfriend. Had the signs always been there, the blatant racism, right under my nose?

Do I even have to ask? Yes, it's been there. Hell, I knew years ago when the little girl who used to play with me was Black, and my mom accused her of stealing from her jewelry box. I knew then but was too young to understand. That little girl was the daughter of our cook, Anita. We used to play hide-n-go-seek, kickball, and so much more. She was my best friend, so when my mom made her leave, I was devastated. And to think, my mom found her diamond bracelet on the floor in the bathroom. But she didn't care that she drug that poor family through the mud. She was just happy that she could. So on that rainy day, I promised myself never to treat anyone less than what they are worth, and I meant that.

I pull into a parking space in the Whitaker Garage. The garage that lives under the City Market area. The last time I was down here, I took two random chicks back to my home, and I haven't been back since in hopes of never running into those girls again.

That would be the straw that breaks the camel's back if Katie found out what happened. I'm literally taking that to my grave...

Once Jade and William find a parking spot, we pile into the elevator, heading up to Ellis Square. Once the doors open, we're assaulted by music, people everywhere, and the smell of weed drifting through the air. When I say it's packed, that's an understatement.

"Wow! Is there an event going on that we don't know about?" Katie asks as we filter through the crowd.

"Shoot, I forgot. It's Orange Crush this weekend," I disclose. After the beach party on Tybee, everyone heads to City Market to hit up the clubs. College students have been spring breaking here for years, and of course the upty people don't want their kind in their neighborhoods. Reminds me of my racist ass mother. Just nasty for no apparent reason. Black people have never done anything wrong to any of us. They have as much right to be in this country as we do. Hell, they never asked to come, we forced them and now we act like we scared of them, well not us. Because I've never been scared of anyone, well except Katie. She'd cut off my balls, and purchase new dogs to feed my balls too.

I shiver just thinking about it...

"Makes sense now," Katie states. "Being out of work keeps me out of the loop."

"Well, let's make the most of it and have a much-needed drink and food," Jade suggests. "I'm starving."

We then head to the Grove and happen to find a cove to sit in and order food and drinks. I can see Katie's tensed shoulders have relaxed a lot since we left my parent's home, but I knew better. I'll undoubtedly hear about it later tonight. I should have never put her in that predicament. But for now, I'll do everything in my power to soothe her uneasiness.

"You wanna dance," I whisper softly in Katie's ear.

"Sure, why not."

She places her palm in my hand, and I guide her to the dance floor. The music switches to 'Murder She Wrote,' by Chaka Demus and Pliers, and I immediately get the show of my life.

The way Katie winds her hips into my dick awakens something in me. I've just realized that I've never actually seen her dance with all of the experiences she has from her past.

The mere effortlessness when she sways herself around me, hypnotizing me with her flawless moves, gives me life. First, I wrap my arms around her as she bends and grinds her ass against my now-stiffened erection. Then, as I slide my hands down her sides, she lifts, running her back down my chest, where I can smell her soporific scent, driving me even wilder than before.

Jesus, I can fuck her right here, right now.

As the music changes, I glance over to my sisters and William, and for the first in my life, I see pure affection spilling my way. They seem happy that I've found happiness, and with that support, I know I can never fail Katie again. I'll always have her back, as she'll always have mine.

"Love, you want another drink, or are you okay?"

"Yeah, I'll take another, but I need to head to the lady's room for a moment. I'll be right back."

When I return to the cove, my sisters begin to grill me.

"You're in love with Katie, aren't you?" Jillian questions.

"What makes you think that?"

"Any fool in this bar can tell by how you look at her. You can't take your eyes off her for even a minute. And the way you defended her at home. You're head over heels in love with her, Jackie," Jade proclaims. "Just admit it."

"Yeah, I am in love with her, and she's with me," I admit.

"I knew it! Why else would you subject her to our crazy family? You wanted a smidge of approval from Mom and Dad, am I right?" Jillian asks.

"Am I wrong for wanting my family to approve of the woman I want to spend the rest of my life with?" I verbalize for the first time.

"No, you're not wrong. But what if Mom never comes around? Then what?" Jade throws out there.

"Then Mom won't be a part of our lives. I won't put Katie through that again. She's right. She's had a hard life, and I'll make it my mission to lessen the heartache if it's the last thing I do."

"We know, and we support any decision you make," Jade offers, and with that, we all hug until I see Katie rushing back to us, her eyes hazed with anger and rage, and I know something is off.

CHAPTER SIXTEEN

KATHERINE

I LEAVE Jackson to get our drinks while I head to the restroom. I have to pee so bad. As I enter the stall, I hear muffled moans in the last one. At first, I pay no mind to it because people fuck in the bathrooms all the time, but then I hear the girl say, please stop. Her voice is off, almost like she's drifting in and out of consciousness.

Oh, hell no. Not on my fucking watch will someone take advantage of a woman in the bathroom.

No fucking way…

I finish my business quickly, wash my hands, and then decide to kick in the fucking door of the stall because why the hell not. Knocking the guy over with his dick hanging out and jeans around his ankles, the girl falls to the ground, between the toilet and the wall.

I then stomp on the guy's head multiple times to knock him out. Not giving him a chance in hell to hurt her or me.

I then help the girl to her feet, and as I take a good look at her. She's wearing a very revealing dress, pulled above her stomach, with no panties on. I notice she's wet between her thighs, with bruising and red markings on her. One of her heels are launched into the toilet. And as I get an even better look at her, she's one of the missing girls. One of the first ones. But shit, I can't remember her name. But I know it's her.

"Wake up, sweetie. Come on, please wake up!" slapping her face firmly but gently to get some life out of her. She's on something, but I have no idea what it is.

I pull my phone out of my back pocket and dial 9-1-1.

The phone rings, and rings before dispatch finally answers the call.

"9-1-1, what's your emergency?" the dispatcher asks.

"Yes, I'm Officer Katherine Harris. I'm at the Grove with a teenage girl who was being raped by a man. I've incapacitated him, but the teen is in and out of consciousness. I think he gave her something. Also, she's one of the missing teens from Saint Vincent's."

"Got it, Harris. I have EMS and officers en route to you."

"I have to pee so bad," a girl states as she rushes into the bathroom. "Oh my gosh! What happened?" She cries out.

"Can you stay with her for just a moment? And make sure he doesn't wake up. I have to get help."

"Sure! Of course."

"Thanks!" I then run out of the restroom and find Jackson.

"Jackson! Baby, I need help."

"What is it?"

"One of the missing girls, she's passed out in the bathroom. I caught a man raping her in one of the stalls."

"Shit!" He stands and follows me closely with his sisters and William behind us. We enter the bathroom, and when we see the girl, I left with the missing girl fighting with the guy on the floor; Jackson pushes me to the side and charges the guy, slamming him into the wall, William right by his side, holding the guy's arms to his sides. Finally, the guy releases the girl from his grasp, and she runs into my arms.

"He was trying to hurt her, and I couldn't...I just—" she cries out.

"It's okay. Everything's okay. We got it from here," I explain to her. I hand her off to Jillian while Jackson holds the guy down, waiting on backup. I splash water on the missing girl's face; it wakes her up just enough to get her name.

"My name is Emma, Emma Bactive, she responds softly."

She then blacks out, and I start CPR to keep her heart pumping and the blood flowing in her veins.

She has to make it. She can't die like this, not like this, and in this moment, I feel pure dread of my own daughter suffering this same fate, and I never got the chance to meet her.

"UM JACK, IS THAT YOU?" THE FRIENDLY GIRL WHO HELPED ask Jackson as I help Emma into the ambulance.

"Uh, do I know you?" Jackson asks her, with confusion and bewilderment in his tone.

"Yeah, remember? We hooked up a couple of weeks ago. Remember, my home girl, Macie and I'm Sara."

What the ever loving fuck?

My glance shifting between the — well, not the nice girl anymore, Sara and Jackson. And in the desperate second that passes between all of us, I see the moment Jackson's recollection of Sara surface to the full front of his f-ing brain.

"Are you fucking kidding me right now?"

"Katie, baby, let me explain," Jackson begs.

"No, no, I can't deal with this shit right now. Emma needs me." I turn my back on him and climb into the ambulance, leaving him, his sisters, and Sara on the side of the road.

I'M AT THE HOSPITAL WITH EMMA WAITING FOR HER MOM'S arrival. The doctors said if we waited any longer, Emma would not be with us today. She was overdosing on Fentanyl, an old-school drug that doctors use for like surgeries and major injuries to manage pain. It resurfaced, sold on the streets, and being used to lace other drugs for a stronger and more intense high.

She's currently resting after the doctor administered a forensic sexual assault kit on her because I witnessed her actively being raped by her assailant. Which, he's now being questioned by SVU.

"Corporal Harris, where's my daughter? How is she doing?" Ms. Bactive fires off, as she enters the emergency room waiting area.

"She's fine physically, resting now. But mentally and emotionally, I'm not sure. We have no idea what she's been through this past week. Not until she's ready to talk, that is," I assure her.

"But she's okay? You sure?" Ms. Bactive questions meekly. I can tell she hasn't slept since her daughter went missing. Not knowing if she's okay, or if she's hurt, or if she's eaten anything. I can only imagine what she's feeling right now.

"Yes, she's fine." And then Ms. Bactive does the unspeakable. She embraces me in a tight hug, and after a moment of shock, I return the hug gratefully.

The doctor approaches us, "Ms. Bactive?"

"Yes. That's me," Ms. Bactive answers.

"Good. Your daughter has woken up and would like to see you."

Tears of joy run down her cheeks, and in that moment, I knew if I hadn't been disrespected by Jackson's mom, Emma would probably be dead. But, like the old saying says, things happen for a reason, and I'm damn glad I suffered harmful words to save a young girl from sticks and stones.

And now that I'm all alone with my dreadful thoughts, all that's occupying my psyche on a constant loop is Jackson fucking not one broad, but two.

I did this. I pushed him in the hands of another woman, actually dick first into two women.

Fuck! Fuck my life right now!

"Katie?" I hear my name being called, but I have yet to acknowledge who it might be.

I don't have time for any of this shit right now.

"Katie," someone calling my name again.

I sit in the waiting room of the ER room, waiting on whatever or whoever.

"That's me," I respond to the unknown person.

"Katie, sweetie, it's me, Jade."

"Jade?" I respond meekly. Because damnit, how the hell am I supposed to feel?

"Yes, honey. I know you may need a ride home and time to process everything that happened today," she explains.

"You don't say?"

"Look, you've been through some fucked up shit and I'm not here to downplay anything or take sides, I'm here to be here, and only here."

"I deserve all of this. I did this to him. I pushed him to his breaking point. Besides, we weren't together when he fucked them. He can do whatever he wants."

"Do you hear yourself?"

"Yeah, I do."

"You can't think that you deserve any of this heartache?" She questions incredulously.

"Of course I do. It's the story of my twisted life. Nothing but bad shit happens to me. Why stop now? Why not add a cheating boyfriend to the mix. Trust me, I've handled a lot worse than this."

"Don't you ever just want life to be different? A life without agony."

"That's not the hand I was dealt."

"You've got to be kidding me?"

"Look, I can find my own ride home. I don't really need you," I explain to her.

"I know you don't need me, I just wanted to offer some support."

"Well, I'm good. Trust me," standing to walk away.

"Actually, I don't think you are and I'm not leaving until you open up. I know you don't know me very well, but you know my brother and to be honest, he's very fond of you, something I've never witnessed from him before. So, I'd like to help in any way I can to help both of you."

"Do you always butt into other people's drama or is it just your brother's you like to interfere in?" Stopping to turn around and face her.

"Ha! Good one. I'm actually finishing up my master's in family therapy. You see, my family isn't the most lovable, as you could tell from tonight, but my bond with my siblings is unbreakable."

"Yeah, I can see that."

"So, what do you say? Can I lend you a ear or a shoulder?"

"Sure." Because if I don't say yes, she'll follow me home anyways.

I'M HOME, IN MY SANCTUARY, WITH JADE, MY CUDDLE BLANKET and a glass of white wine to chase the demons away.

"So, masters hun? Does your family know you're completing your master's degree?" Jackson has never mentioned Jade going to school.

"Not exactly."

"Yeah, I figured. Jackson never mentioned it. So, why are you hiding?"

"Well, because I've never really finished anything and I didn't want to let them down once again."

"So, already doubting yourself before you even try, sounds a bit familiar?"

"Kettle, meet pot. You'd love her…" she mocks me, as I throw a pillow at her. "Hey," catching the pillow before it hits her face.

"Look, I've had a pretty wretched experience in life, you don't know the half of it. And I put your brother through a lot. I'm really not surprised he went looking for something elsewhere. I damn near threw him into Sara's lap. How can I be mad?"

"I'm not saying that you should, but it had to hurt, just a little," squeezing her index finger and thumb together to show emphasis.

"You're right. It did hurt. Finding out that way, but I'm not mad. I just needed space. To think, get my thoughts together."

"I get it and I think my brother will understand, but right now, he thinks you're walking away, giving up on what y'all have worked so hard to have. He thinks it's over."

"No, he can't possibly think that. I'd never leave him again, but he probably should leave me. Find someone who will make him happy, someone who won't add gloominess to his shine. He deserves so much more than I can offer him. He deserves so much more than me…"

"You know what? That's a load of horse shit and you know it. He literally worships the ground you walk. Did you know the entire time y'all was separated, he mopped around like a sad puppy dog. Even when our mother tried to set him up, he refused to date any of them because he knew what he wanted."

"And what's that?"

"Seriously…you, Katie. He wanted you."

"I—I don't know what to say to that."

"Don't say anything. Get off your ass and go get your man."

IT'S LATE, LIKE VERY LATE AND I'M STATIONED OUTSIDE Jackson's door, apprehensively debating if I should knock or leave. My heart is racing a thousand miles a minute and my stomach cramping something fierce.

Damnit, I should just walk away. I can't do this. What if he rejects me like I rejected him so many times before?

What if he laughs in my face and send me skittering away with my tail tucked between my legs?

What if—God, what if he has had enough?

I turn to walk away when I hear the familiar clicking of the lock. It's so deafening, I can't process anything else. Not the words spoken behind me, not the crickets chirping in the meadow, not the frogs crowing, mocking me, teasing me.

"Katie, love, baby?" I hear in the very near distance. "Katherine, please turn to me," I feel him tugging on my hand gently.

"I'm so sorry Jackson. I—I didn't...what I mean to say—"

"Katie, you have nothing to apologize for. I'm the one that should be apologizing. I've made a grave mistake and I wish I could take it back, but I can't."

"Hold on," silencing him with a simple touch to his soft lips. "I'm not mad. I know I pushed you too far and for that, I'm terribly sorry for the way I've treated you. You don't deserve any of it."

Lifting my chin, to gaze in his summerly mysterious evergreens dancing in the deep of the forest on a bright night. His eyes tell a story of passion and curiosity.

Cupping my cheeks in his palms, lifting me on my toes and he places the simplest kiss on my lips. This kiss is so tender and loving, something I've never experienced before. This kiss is accepting me, all of me, my flaws, my fears, my scars. This kiss is absorbing all of me.

I spade my palms across his chiseled firm back, pulling him closer to me. I need to feel him, touch him, make love to him.

"Please take me inside, Jackson." And that's all the invitation he needs. No more worries, no more doubts, no more anything because I know if any man is willing to cut ties with his mom to love me, I know I have a good man by my side, and I couldn't ask for more.

I have a real one. Most women spend their entire lives in search of a man who will treat them right; with respect. And I don't have to because in ever action he displays in front of me and the world, is meant to care for me.

He respects my boundaries and never forces me into anything I'm not ready for. He asks me how my day is and genuinely cares about the answer. He makes protecting my heart a priority and he's never confused of where I stand in his life.

As he guides me to his bedroom, he's taking one item off of me at a time, exposing my scars, my dark skin, my plumped and swollen breast that are aching for his touch, his mouth, his everything.

He lifts me in his arms, and carries me to his bed, gently lying me on top of his plush spread.

He stands over me, watching me, cataloging every inch of me.

As he lifts his shirt over his head, I gasp at the mere sight of his milky body displayed before me. And when he drops his sweats and boxers on the floor, I nearly combust and he haven't even entered me yet.

He leans over me, careful not to hurt me in any way, taking my nipple into his mouth, sucking with such purpose, I cry out in pure ecstasy.

Jackson thrust his fingers into me, milking my pleasure over and over again.

I arch into his hand, desperate for more.

I *need* more.

"Please…" I beg for more.

And without another thought, Jackson fills me, thrusting harder and harder, then softly and methodically slower, and lord knows I couldn't ask for a better feeling as he depletes his essence into my very soul.

JACKSON AND I LAY IN EACH OTHER'S EMBRACE FOR HOURS AS I watch the sun arise in the distance. I love the view from his bedroom window. Nothing like the view I see every morning from mine.

In this very moment, I know the next decision I make will tear him apart, but he will accept my decision and stand by my side no matter what, because he loves me and I love him.

NICOLETTE JOHNSON

That's why I know now I must help find the rest of the girls, and I must do it sooner than later. My new mission in life, whether it kills me or not.

First things first, I must meet Bobby. He's the key to this mess, and I must face my past whether I want to or not.

CHAPTER SEVENTEEN

JACKSON

I AWAKEN to my dick being sucked, nibbled, stroked, fondled, and Jesus Christ, it's a glorious feeling. Katie is fucking great at giving head, and I'd be damned if I gave this up every morning.

She wraps her plushed lips around the length of my shaft, sucking hard and then licking the bulging vein nearing my balls. She cradles them in her delicate grip while twirling them in her grasp. This wake-up call feels so good; I don't want her to stop. She cups my balls in her tiny hands once again while bitting a little more on my head, giving me an intense feeling in my core.

I grunt out incoherent words letting her know I'm damn near close, never coming so soon in my life. She doesn't heed my warning when I spill my cum between those full soft sexy as fuck lips. Taking me in like it's the only meal she'll have and fuck yeah, I owe her the same pleasure, flipping her over onto her back, running my fingers over her swollen clit and impale her with my middle and ring finger, curving into her, making her buck for more. I take her throbbing clit into my mouth and fuck her with my tongue and fingers, demanding orgasms from her inner core.

"Give it to me, Love. You know you want to," I tease, and at that very moment, she releases her pleasure for my appraisal. "That's it, Love. That's it baby girl."

Crying out my name is pure ecstasy; I climb on top of her, and glide my length over her moist clit, giving me much-needed lube. I then thrust into her swiftly and hard.

"Oh, God, Jackson!" she cries out. And I know she wants me to fuck her hard and fast. Hell, we both need it rough, and I'm willing to give her everything I got and more.

I thrust and thrust, then slide out slowly, forcing her to use her heels to push me back in. She's such a needy girl, and I love it. I thrust again, swirling my hips to match each thrust, and the moment I know she's close, I slam into her unapologetically, forcing her to squirt all over my dick, and in a moment's time, I come one more time, depleting me completely. But before I collapse on her, I catch myself on my forearms, and roll to the side, bringing her with me without sliding out of her.

I can do this forever.

Feathering my calloused fingertips over her skin, I feel her relax in my embrace, but I can tell something is bothering her.

"What's worrying that pretty head of yours?" I ask as I softly kiss her temple. She's forgiven me for the most unforgivable mistake; she could ask me to alter the moon and I'd do just that to protect her from the world without a second thought.

"I keep thinking about those girls. Are they suffering the same fate as Emma? Am I too late? Have we not done enough?" The questions come pouring out, and I just sit because I know there isn't a wrong or right answer. She needs to talk this out. "Jackson, I want, no, I need to find Bobby."

"Who's Bobby?" I inquire.

"He's my old boss from the strip club."

"Oh, that guy," I tense at the mention of the club.

"Yeah, I know he knows where to start with finding them, and the only way to get through to him is approaching him on his territory."

"Katie, I don't like where this is going," I state firmly.

"I know. But I have to try. I know I can get through to him."

"But, why does it have to be you? Why not let SVU bring him in?"

"Because I know the operation better than anyone. If I don't know anything else, I know he has those girls or knows where to find them, and I have to help them."

Knowing I can do nothing to sway her decision, I give in. "Fine, but I want to help."

"Deal!" She agrees before I can change my mind, and I know she'd probably go with or without me anyways.

THE NEXT MORNING, KATIE AND I ENTER SGT. MAUI'S OFFICE, ready to help in any way we can.

"Hi, Sarge. I'm ready," Katie offers proudly.

"Perfect! Have a seat," Sgt. Maui gestures to the chairs in front of her desk. "I know this may be difficult for you, but any help you can offer will make a wave of difference.

"I know what it's like to be alone and scared. I don't wish that on anyone, and if I can do anything to ease a young girl's mind or save her from her demise, I'm down for whatever you need," Katie poses.

"Well, we need someone in that club, someone who's familiar with the layout, the day-to-day activities, the ins and outs."

I see Katie tense a little, and know she wasn't expecting what Sarge is proposing.

"What are you asking?" I speak up.

"Harris, we need you to go undercover to find anything that can lead us to the rest of the missing girls," Sgt. Maui discloses.

"Undercover? In what capacity?" Katie asks.

"To put it bluntly, stripping," Sgt. Maui answers.

"I'm not sure I can go back in there like that; not like that," Katie meekly states. "I know I have to talk to Bobby, but I didn't think I'd be undercover, stripping. That's a lot to ask," Katie admits.

"I know it is, but it's our only way of finding the girls," Sgt. Maui verbalizes, and I see the genuine concern in her features, "But, if—"

"No, I know you're right. I'll do it," Katie surrenders quicker than I thought she would. She never really talked about what went down in that place other than what the video captured, and now, I see that it's way more than she led on before, and I don't know if I can handle putting her in that situation again, whatever it is.

"Katie, are you sure about this?" I ask.

"No, I'm not. But I don't have a choice."

"You do have a choice. You always have a choice. Let someone else go in, and you guide them through wiretapping or whatever."

"Bobby will see straight through them. It has to be me. Besides, he always said I'd be crawling back to him. So, this is me crawling and then nailing his sorry, worthless ass to the wall," Katie expresses proudly.

"Thank goodness! We'll get you wired up and ready tonight," Sgt. Maui states.

"No wires," Katie responds.

"Over my dead cold body! You will, and there's no debate about that," I deadpan.

"What I mean is, Bobby will have me searched. Can you put a camera or something on my necklace? It's my mom's, and Bobby knows I never take it off," Katie conveys softly, spinning the pendant between her fingers. I've seen her twirl her necklace in her fingers when she's nervous, or unsure about something.

"Yeah, that would work," Sgt Maui answers.

Katie takes the necklace off and hands it over to the surveillance guy from the IT department. I've seen him a lot at the precinct. "Please be careful. That's the only thing I have of my mom's," Katie expresses.

"I'll take good care of it. So don't worry," the guy reassures.

I have a terrible fucking feeling about this, but I know I don't have an up in this dog fight. Katie must do this to leave her past in the past. She must face her fears, the worries that have held her hostage for fifteen long years.

CHAPTER EIGHTEEN

KATHERINE

I'M SITTING in my apartment, trying to wrap my mind around the shit I just offered myself to. Then, standing abruptly, shaking every limb, loosing every muscle I have, "YOU GOT THIS!" telling myself in my floor-length mirror. It's nothing like self-motivation.

You can face the devil that tormented you for fifteen years. Who took the most precious thing from you, who took your strength and stomped on it like roaches scathing by.

"Kathrine Nicole Harris, you can do this!"

I walk into my room and into my closet. I reach for a box; a box I haven't opened in years. The black box contains all the costumes I wore so long ago. Outfits, I probably can't even fit anymore, but the smaller and skimpier they are, the better...

I ruffle through until I find a multi-colored neon see-through bra and G-string. The colors will look flawless and vibrant against my dark skin, but only one thing I've forgotten about…my scars.

These scars are only for my eyes to see, well, Jackson's too, but now so many people will see how flawed I am, and that alone scares the hell out of me.

But I made a promise and must follow through for the girls' sake.

I put on the bra and panties, with washed-out cut-up jean shorts and a cut-up tank. I wear four-inch heels, style my hair, apply neon makeup, and head out the door to meet Jackson, Sgt. Maui and the rest of the team.

"You got this!"

"Whoa! You look—totally different?" Sgt. Maui praises. "You'll fit right in."

Don't I know it, but can I climb that pole again… we shall see.

"Here's your necklace, ready to record," the tech guy hands me, hesitantly.

"Here, I'll help you," Jackson offers. Unfortunately, he's been reticent through this whole ordeal. I know he's bothered by all of this, but this is something I have to do.

"Thank you," I express wholeheartedly. Because if it weren't for his strength and relaxed nature, I genuinely don't think I'd be able to do any of this.

He places my necklace around my neck, brushing his fingers across my skin, causing goose bumps to flare. Then, placing a gentle kiss at the base of the precious jewel, he nervelessly turns me around and stares into my eyes with those mossy green irises with slender strands of gold-like spikes around a pinwheel. His eyes tell a story, a fantasy that can't be described with words but feeling.

His palm sets on my cheek, and I lean into his caress, needing so much more than just a touch. I need everything in this moment.

He lifts my chin to gently kiss my lips, but I pull him forward, needing more than just a peck. I need a deep passion that can only be told by us. I need an out-of-body experience that only he can give me. I need so much more than what he's giving me, but I know I must wait.

"Ready?" Sgt. Maui asks as she sticks her head into the room. We haven't been very open about our relationship, but we're not trying to hide either. I know I was trying to establish boundaries, but realistically, why do I even bother?

These past two years have been a whirlwind, I've really grown beyond my past. I've faced things I normally wouldn't, and it feels good; it feels blissful, life-affirming. I can breathe like actually breathe.

"Yes, I'm ready," I respond reluctantly, more so because I don't want to lose this closeness from Jackson. "I'll be out in just a minute."

"You know you can walk away right now. No one will hold it against you. And I'd be right behind you," Jackson states begrudgingly.

"And not face my fears, my nightmares, my reality?"

"Shit, I didn't—I'm just—"

"I know. You're worried. Hell, I am too. But if we don't find those girls, their fate can be worse than mine was, and I don't wish that on anyone."

"I understand. I do." He kisses me firmly on my forehead, and I lean in, desperately needing support. He pulls away from our embrace, stares into my eyes, and then walks away, turning his back to me, and at that moment, I wish I could fade away...

I ENTER THE NIGHTCLUB THAT HOUSES THE FEARS I'VE endured most of my adult life. It's dark, with black fluorescent lights shadowing above me. I see a sizeable burly man at the closed door, the door that allows you to enter your fantasies. He's tall, muscular, dressed in all black with his arms crossed in front of him like he'll rip me apart if I tried anything.

"Can I help you?" the Bouncer states firmly in such a deep voice, if I were as weak as I was fifteen years ago, I'd piss my pants.

"Yes, I'm here to see Bobby."

"And who's asking?"

"Clarity Rose!"

"Boss, a Clarity Rose here to see you," the Bouncer states in an earpiece. Moments later, the door opens, and I'm ushered into the club. A tall, slender man on the other side of the door greets me and then escorts me through the open door. He's not as intimidating as the bouncer at the door. Probably by design, to drop my guard.

There are girls on poles dancing to the music, swaying from top to bottom. Girls swinging from the ceiling, wearing nothing but G-strings or thongs. There're girls held up in secluded areas with men surrounding them. Three female bartenders in the middle of the club, surrounded by a sphere bar top with men watching their every move, because why not... they're completely naked with nothing on but a bowtie.

The slender guy guides me through mirrored glass doors, and as they shut behind me, I realize they are one-way mirrors. You can see out, but no one can see in. On the opposite side of the room, an older Black man sits with two girls draped on his arms. With a full, fluffy beard, bald head, and earrings the size of tiny fists in both ears, he stares at me with a mucky smirk. As if he knew this day would come…one day.

You'd think I'd focus on the girls on each of his arms because they are way too young, but nope. Instead, I'm fixated on the large husky man in the middle, commanding my attention, no, demanding it.

He finally speaks, startling me for a moment. I hadn't realized I was staring, nor did I hear the slender man leave behind me.

"Sit, Clarity Rose." I do as I'm told, grasping my necklace around my neck, forgetting a camera is in it, "What can I do for you?"

"I need help," I respond meekly.

"Speak up; I can't hear you," Bobby demands.

"I need your help," I state firmly with a little more backbone.

"You. Need. My help. Whatever for?" He taunts me. But I set my pride aside and stand firm to the mission at hand.

He can't hurt you anymore. I tell myself.

"I need to make quick money."

"And what makes you think I can help you?"

"Because you're always looking for girls to dance, service, or bartend. I can do whatever; I just need the money."

"For what?'

"Huh?"

"What do you need the money for, Clarity Rose?"

"I owe someone money."

"For what?" he questions suspiciously.

"Uh... I've been trying to start a family, have a kid, and the IBFs are beyond expensive, so I borrowed money from the wrong person, and now if I don't pay him, he's—" not finishing the statement, allowing fake tears to flow down my cheeks.

"Baby girl, don't cry. I always said I had you. You're the one who left."

"Because—"

"You know you have to give a little to get a little. You know my rules."

"Yes, but—they hurt me badly; I was scared."

"And I took care of you afterward. Paid your medical bills, and then you just up and left... you left me. How am I supposed to take that? You know I don't let just anyone leave... there's consequences."

Taking a deep breath, "And I'm ready to face those consequences if you'd allow me a month to work off my debt."

"A month, huh? What's the debt?"

"Eighty stacks."

"And you think a month will pay off that?" he asks incredulously.

"I was hoping..."

"Can you still climb the pole?"

"Uh, I'm not sure... it's been a while."

"Fifteen years..." he deadpans. Staring at me so intensely. "Look, I need to see what my investment is," he finally speaks after moments of eye fucking me.

I place my purse on the floor with a soft thud. I then start sliding my jean shorts down and lift my shirt above my head, dropping both in a heap. And just then, my scars begin to pulsate, forgetting that my flaws might just end all of this.

"There, your investment," I spit out. I hate this part, but I knew it was coming. He always has to validate his investments.

He approaches me with lustful eyes, licking his lips with such desire in every stride. I brace myself for whatever is next.

He runs his firm fingers across my skin, and I silently apologize to Jackson because I know he's enduring every excruciating moment behind the scenes.

"Your battle scars give you a certain allure, and I'm getting hard just thinking about what I can do to you, with you…." Bobby whispers softly in my ear, but I know the team can hear every word of my demise.

"I thought you would enjoy seeing your handy work," admitting to everyone the very person who hurt me all those years ago is standing behind me.

Because it wasn't just a group of guys raping me, it was him. It was him with the razor blade. He's the monster I've been running away from all those years ago.

It was HIM.

"I'll bring you back," snapping me back to reality. "But only for my entertainment, my pleasure," twirling my pendant in his fingers. "I see you never took this off."

"Yeah, remember. It's my mother's."

"Awe, yes. How could I forget," snapping my head back and deep throat kissing me.

And I know right then and there I have no choice but to agree to his terms.

CHAPTER NINETEEN

JACKSON

I WATCH as he drags his slimy, filthy hands down Katie's body—no, my body. Her fucking body belongs to me, not that sick son-of-a-bitch!

And kissing her—my lips. Her lips are mine.

Just watching this fucking scene unfold has me on the fucking edge. If I could just make all of this shit stop, I would.

"Wow, she got this undercover thing down pack," one of the investigators says out loud. Really not knowing which one said that fucked-up shit. I'm seething beyond control, shaking through my anger.

"Yeah, Sarge, we get it now. We see why you've worked so hard to get her in this unit. She got me convinced."

"Got you convinced of what?" I seethed between clenched teeth.

"That she's been doing this all her life. Look at that performance. She didn't even flinch when he wanted to look at his investments," the guy explains, throwing up air quotes around his investments.

I take deep breaths and don't even realize I have Sarge rubbing my back softly. "Maybe you should sit this one out," Sgt. Maui suggests quietly. "I know this can be very difficult to watch, with y'all being partners and all." I glance at her over my shoulder because we both know that's a loaded statement. "Listen, I'm not here to mess things up for you two, but you need to think long and hard if you're able to endure the shit that's about to go down."

"What? Why would you say that?"

"Because I understand the lingo, but you might not. And I know you and Harris got something going on. Wait before you speak. Here me out." I take a breath, something I didn't think I was holding. She's right. I have to hear her out whether I want to or not. I gesture for her to continue. "Thank you. I've done my background on Harris. I know what she's been through. I know the trauma she's suffered and that I'm putting her in an impossible position, to face all of it again. But what you don't know is I've been investigating Bobby for over fifteen years, and I truly know what happened to her. She's my only valuable victim, and it's my job to convince her to come forward. She doesn't know I've been investigating that whole operation, and when the girls started showing up missing, I knew he had his hand in it somehow. I just couldn't prove it."

"But what does this have to do with Katie?"

"She knows more than she thinks. I truly believe she blocked most of the trauma from her psyche. She knows she was hurt but blocked who did it to her."

"She said she would have nightmares. Do you think she's reliving the trauma through her dreams?"

"It's a possibility. I'd have to get an expert to talk with her."

"I'm not so sure about that. She's a very private person."

"Yes, I know. But I believe after doing this, she'll need it whether I order her to get help or she does it on her own."

"I understand, but what I want to know is what's about to go down, and I mean, I need to know every excruciating detail."

"Are you sure you want to know?"

"Unquestionably certain!"

CHAPTER TWENTY
KATHERINE

I CLIMB the pole with fragile precision. I'm not as flexible as I used to be, but I'm able to jump back in with a little effort.

I wrap my legs around the pole and twirl with the music, reminding myself, I got this. As I twist with less effort than before, I find myself enjoying this natural pleasure. I'm not only pleasing Bobby, but I'm also gratifying myself. I'm openly enjoying every minute of this performance. I didn't realize I'd missed this so much.

I focus my gaze on one of the young girls on the couch. Her features are alluring yet familiar. I can't really put my finger on it just yet, but I've seen her before. She looks pale and a little disoriented.

As I continue my performance for Bobby, I focus on the other girl. Now, I know she can't be no more than fifteen. Maybe thirteen with a lot of makeup. Her hair is draped over her shoulders, matting to her skin. Her makeup is so heavy it's sliding off with every swipe she makes to her cheeks. I see drool slide down her lips, and at that moment, I know she's on something.

I try hard to refocus and not fall the hell off this pole when the music stops.

Bobby gives me a standing ovation with a booming applause. I slide down and gracefully bow in front of him.

"My Clarity Rose! You're finally back home," Bobby gushes, and I just want to vomit.

He takes my hand and guides me to the opposite couch of the young girls.

"I'm glad you're luxuriated in my performance. I couldn't have done it without your appraises."

"Non-sense. You were born to entertain. You sway with such flawless precision, hypnotizing your audience. You're going to make me a ton of money, and I know just how to present you to the world."

CHAPTER TWENTY-ONE
JACKSON

AS KATIE SWAYS around the pole, I can't help but think why she's never shown that side of her to me? Is she ashamed? Does she think I'll be upset?

If it weren't for the mirrors in the room, I'd think this was just a ruse, something just to make me believe she wasn't literally gliding in the air with just a G-string and neon colorful bra. A see through bra at that. I now see what Bobby sees in her. She's perfection. She's exquisitely talented. She's every man's wet dream and more.

How could I not see this before? How could I be so blind?

"He's going to want to try his investment," Sgt. Maui states.

"What do you mean by that?" Because I need her to spell it out for me.

"He's going to fuck her whether she want to or not."

"And you're just going to let it happen?" I ask incredulously.

"We have to find all three girls."

"What the actual—?"

"Can you pause this screen?" Sgt. Maui asks, cutting me off and pointing to the far-left screen of the room. Getting out of my own head, I see there are five screens set up with different viewpoints. The screen Sarge is referring to shows two girls on a couch in the same room as Katie. They look out of it or on something. Something seems vaguely familiar about them, but I can't put my finger on it. "Yes, that's it. Now zoom in a little," Sgt. Maui instructs.

As the screen zooms in, I see what she sees. The girls, "Those are two of the missing girls, Maya Hernandez and Vivian Blanchard. But where is the other," I ask the unspoken question.

"That's what we need to find out, and now, it's up to Harris to find her."

CHAPTER TWENTY-TWO
KATHERINE

BOBBY LEAVES me in the room with the two girls. And from the looks of it, they are going in and out of consciousness.

"Hey, my name is Clarity. What is yours?" I ask both.

"Uh—uh, um, Maya. Maya Hernandez." Right, she's one of the missing girls we've looking for.

"I'm Viv—Vivian. Vivian Blanchard. Are you here to help us?"

I shh them because I ain't stupid. Bobby has cameras everywhere in this room, whether you can see them or not. "What do you mean?" I ask instead.

"I don't wanna be here anymore," Vivian whines.

"I'm so cold," Maya states meekly.

"It'll be okay."

The door opens, and the girls shift closer together in pure fear.

"Bobby, let me get these girls something to eat and get them cleaned up for you. They're no good to you if they're deprived," I state firmly.

"See, this is why I need you. I know nothing about bitches. And my wife is useless, spending all my money and nothing to show for it," Bobby barks. "You know where the cleaning room is. Take them there," he demands, waving me off.

He's married? Who the hell would marry a sleez ball like him?

I try lifting the girls on their feet, but it's no use. They are completely out of it. "Can one of the guards help me?" I ask, praying I'm not showing too much of who I've become.

And out of nowhere, he slaps both on the legs with a whip. It happens so fast; it catches me off guard, causing me to stumble back. The sound alone is deafening.

The girls jolt completely straight, ready to move at command. Shit, what has he been doing to these girls?

Vivian and Maya walk independently; well, I wouldn't exactly call it walking, more like shuffling across the floor with no more hope or flame in their movement. But at least their moving.

I've got to get them out of here…but how?

I really hope SVU is seeing all of this…

We need the calvary now!

CHAPTER TWENTY-THREE

JACKSON

"WE GOTTA GET them the fuck out of there! Did you see what he just did to them?" I bellow, feeling beyond useless right now. This shit is for the birds. I have to help Katie, and, now! 'Cause I'll be damned if I have to sit here and watch that fucker hurt her in any way.

"Harris knows what she's doing. We cannot jeopardize this investigation, not now, and we not pulling her. She has to find Serenity; we'll pull all of them when she does. But, for now, sit down and don't say another word, comprender?" And even though I know nothing about Spanish other than Hola and Adios, I understood precisely what is expected of me, and that's why I have to get the fuck out of here and now.

There's no way I'm sitting here and just going to watch Katie get hurt or, worse, die

There's no fucking way...

CHAPTER TWENTY-FOUR

KATHERINE

WE MAKE it down the dark hall to the cleaning room, also known as the ass-chewing room. Back in the day, the house mistress would beat us senseless to prove her fucking point. Sometimes, I'd think she was jealous because she could no longer do what we could. I remember Jazzy getting it the worse, always talking back and disobeying her orders. I think Jazzy did most of that to piss the mistress off. What was her name again? Shit, I had no idea I forgot so much about this place.

As I enter the room, I notice some things have been changed, like the color of the walls. They used to be bright red but are now a soft sage color. The furniture has been upgraded to velvety plush lounges, and the dressing rooms have doors, like actual doors. The walls have floor-length mirrors, and the vanity tables are modern-style chic.

I never thought I'd witness such impeccable taste in this hell hole in a million years, but then again, I thought Bobby would kill me dead right where I stood the moment he saw me.

Things can certainly change...

As the girls flop down on the sofas, I head to the bathroom to run some hot water for both of them. As I enter the room, I hear a faint breathing sound in one of the stalls. So, of course, me being me, I investigate.

I open the last stall in the corner and see a girl bleeding severely from several cuts on her body. She's completely naked and frail. I rush to her side, trying to see what I can do to help her, but she moans loudly when I try to move her. She must have some broken bones as well.

As I turn her a little, I have a clearer view of her face, "Oh, goodness, Serenity? No, no, no, please God," I silently pray. Please let her be okay. "It's okay. I'm going to get you out of here," I promise her, but not really sure I can even keep it.

She coughs something back, but it's mumbled. I leave her and then rush to the other room to see what I can use to cleanse her wounds.

As I enter, I run directly into Jazzy.

CHAPTER TWENTY-FIVE

JACKSON

BY THE GRACE OF GOD, I've managed to slip out of SVU, maneuver through the windy halls, and make it outside without being noticed by the team. They're so engorged in the operation; it'll take them a while to register my absence.

I decide to take my personal car instead of the largely labeled marked unit. It's about a thirty-minute drive to the club, so I take this time to try to develop a plan. Something, anything to get Katie, the girls, and I out safely.

But nothing...not a fucking thing comes to mind. Fuck, slamming my fist on the steering wheel.

Turning on the Apple Play, Neva Eva by Trillville, featuring Lil Scrappy and Lil Jon, blasts through the Bose speakers I've installed recently, putting me in that state of mind... "Get on my Level, hoe, get on my level, hoe," I rap aggressively in my car because I don't give a fuck right now.

NICOLETTE JOHNSON

I head to the bank teller to get some cash. Strip clubs are not known to take credit cards. After retrieving the max amount from three different banks, I pull into the parking lot, hyping myself up. I check my wallet; I have close to three grand on me. Can't go in there empty-handed. Sure hope they got change for twenties.

I step out of the car, approach the entrance, and stand in line behind all the other horny dudes, waiting to get a glimpse of what's inside.

After waiting for what feels like forever, it's my turn to be searched by the bodyguard at the front. Once he violates me in every fucking way, I make it through the doors…

Scanning the open dark room with neon strobing lights, I search for any signs of Katie. Finally, I make my way to the bar and start a tab. I'm immediately approached by a pale girl, slim, with big tits and literally nothing on but a thong. She's physically fit, just not my style, but I go along with it anyway to keep up appearances.

As she approaches, I hand her a twenty for a quick lap dance, still scanning the room of my surroundings.

I notice movement in the hallway leading to the back and focus on that area. Once I see two women fighting, one is Katie, and the other, I'm unfamiliar with; my sole thought process is to push the blonde girl off me and help my love, my angel.

And I do just that!

CHAPTER TWENTY-SIX

KATHERINE

"JAZZY, WHAT ARE YOU DOING HERE?" I ask, thoroughly confused.

"I should be asking the same thing," she responds with a hint of disgust.

"I've come to speak with Bobby, and I'm trying to get these girls cleaned up," not leading on the real reason I'm there. I need to figure out what the fuck is going on and now.

"Well, my husband and I own the club," she deadpans.

"Your husband… owns the club?"

"Yeah, we both do. I believe you know who he is?" she teases.

"Uh, am I supposed to?"

"You know, for you to have finished school, found life and all, and became a cop, you're sure, is dumb. But, okay, if you must know, Bobby is my husband."

"What?" I utter in disbelief. She must be who Bobby was referring to earlier.

Damn, makes sense now.

"Yeah! After you finally left, because, let's face it, you were his little beloved, but whatever. After you left, I became his prize. Giving him everything he ever wanted and needed. He fucks me, and only me, and that's how it should be. But now, you walks back in, and he got a fucking hard-on for you, not me!" she spits out. I hear faint sounds from Serenity and Vivian, and Maya isn't far behind her. I gotta get them out of here.

"Listen, Jazzy. I really don't want Bobby. You can have him. I'm just trying to make extra money to pay my debt. That's all. Now can you help with these girls or what?"

"Fuck them, hoes. They tried to steal Bobby too. So they get whatever the fuck they deserve," she spits out, and right at that moment, I know I'm dealing with a deranged woman and not the Jazzy I knew fifteen years ago.

"Do you really think Bobby only has eyes for you? He runs a strip club, for heaven's sake," I spit out.

"I knew his eyes wondered. Hell, when I found that video of him and his boys fucking you, I had no choice but to release it to the world. Make you pay for making my life a living hell while you were still here. You know he wanted me to be the entertainment on that night. But, Mistress had other plans. She beat the bricks off me that night and I finally had enough. I killed her, nice and slow, snatching that whip from her grasp and bestowing the same fate she bestowed upon me. She was a piece of work. After much convincing, and of course framing you for killing dear old Mistress, Bobby thought you would be a better choice. Earn more money. And pay for taking his precious hag away from him."

Paralyzed with anger, I growl like actually growl at her.

And before I know it, Jazzy is launching toward me at full speed with a sick and twisted look plastered on her face. I sidestep to avoid collision and maneuver Jazzy away from the other girls.

She comes for me again, but this time I swing her to the other side of the room and then take off running out of the door, leaving the girls and Jazzy.

As I approach the door, Jazzy has caught up to me, trying to pull at the little bit of hair I got and clawing at me with her long nails.

I'm not trying to fight this girl over no man, but she's the cause of me and Jackson's breakup. She's the cause of the torment I endured for no reason at all other than pure jealousy and right now I must put her in her place. And after she scrapes at my eyes, I slam her on the ground outside the door in the hallway. I then commence to beatin' her ass.

I'm so sick of people taking my weakness for kindness. "I'm sick of bitches like you," slamming her head into the ground over and over again. Then, while taking all my frustration out on Jazzy, someone who deserves to be beaten to a pulp, I feel hands on my shoulders, snatching me hard and roughly. I turn my fury on the unknown person.

Once I spin around, I see Bobby lifting me off the ground and throwing me over his shoulder. I squeal loudly and try to get down. I believe I see Jackson as I struggle, but it can't be. He's not here. He wouldn't step foot in a slimy place like this, not for me. My eyes are definitely deceiving me.

But then I hear his voice. That voice I crave to hear every waken moment, knowing now it's not a dream. He's really here, and he's here to help me. But wait. He can't. Bobby won't give two fucks about who he is; he will kill him if he tries anything. So, I wave him off, "Please, not now. Please wait," I mouth to him. And he stops and grabs a female nearby, flashing some bills in her face, and she gives him what he's paying for.

I can't be furious that he'd put his hands on another chick, I won't be. I'm only glad that he listened to me. I rather he fuck some broad then watch him be killed because that's exactly what Bobby would do.

Bobby burst through the door and toss me on a makeshift bed. "Who the fuck told you, you can put your hands on my wife?" he demands.

"I didn't know she was your wife, and she came at me," I shoot back.

"You'll have to be punished."

"For what? I didn't do anything. She should've never come for me sideways. Besides, I fight back. I'm not that pathetic little girl anymore," I snap back.

"Bring her in," he states to the guy standing in the corner. The guy I didn't even realize was there.

"Yes, sir." He then walks out, and moments later, he brings Serenity's fragile body into the room, dropping her on the bed next to me.

She cries out in pain and it takes everything in me not to comfort her.

"Either you're punished, or your precious daughter will receive the same fate as you. Your choice."

Shit, I can't let that happen whether she's mine or not. No one should have to endure the hell I've been through. Nobody.

Hold on, how does he know she's my daughter? I don't even know that bit of info yet.

"She's not my daughter," I explain cautiously.

"Kathrine, do you think I'm stupid," he spits out, using my real name. I never once told him my real name.

"No, I don't, but I swear. I don't know who this girl is and my name is Clarity Rose," I try to persuade.

"Drop the fucking act," he spits out.

"I swear I just found her and she wasn't doing so well, so I tried helping her, and then Jazzy came in and attacked me for fucking you or coming back, whatever she was blabbering about...."

Smack! A brutal hit to the side of my face sending hot pain through my cheek. Smack! Again and again and again.

I ball into a fetal position, trying my best to protect my face. He destroyed my body. I can't give him my face too. Not that!

And before he can deliver another slap, I block his hit, finding strength I stand, and throw one hell of a punch to the side of his face and then side-chop him in the throat with my forearm. He doubles down, but before he hits the floor, the bodyguard comes at me with his gun.

I sidestep again, snatching the gun from the bodyguard, disarming him before he can even register what happened. I pull the trigger, shooting the bodyguard first. Then I aim the gun at Bobby, my nightmare, the devil of my dreams, the father of my child.

He holds his hands up in surrendering to his fate.

"You bastard. You fuck, boy. For fifteen fucking years, you've had me paralyzed in your control. Not no fucking mo." I place my finger on the trigger, prepared to pull at any moment, when I hear the door open and officers ordering me to put the gun down.

I don't listen at first, stuck in my rut, my impetuous zone, ready to end all my fears.

These people, especially Bobby has truly fucked my life. Why should I even care about them living? Why?

"Katie, love. Please put the gun down," I hear Jackson encourage me with a gentle voice. A wave of relief washes over me, and I so want to put the gun down, but I can't. This prick deserves to die.

"I don't know if I can do that."

"Yes, you can love, and you will."

NICOLETTE JOHNSON

"This sick son go a bitch has tormented me for years, holding my fate and future in his twisted, demented control. Causing me to watch over both shoulders, never trusting anyone. He deserves to die like the fucking dog he is. He must die! So he won't hurt anyone else. I can't let him hurt anyone else, ever!" I spur out in defeated heartache.

He approaches me slowly as the tears spill over my eyelashes. His arm is wrapped in a scarf, and I wonder what happened to him. He's hurt, broken, and even then, he's trying to soothe me. Trying to care for me. He then takes the gun into his free hand and wraps his arm around my shoulders, bringing me in for an intense embrace. And I break completely down as people all around us, rushing, handcuffing, providing aid, and I just realize that I'm damn near naked in front of all my peers.

Oh well, now they know I'm hard because I have to be, not because I want to be.

CHAPTER TWENTY-SEVEN
JACKSON

WATCHING that dick toss Katie over his shoulder like a sack of potatoes got my blood boiling. He got to her before I could, and now I have to watch this debacle unfold. The moment Katie waved me off, I knew it was a bad fucking idea to just walk away. So, I do what I should have done the first time; I call in the calvary. They're thirty minutes out, which is the dumbest shit ever. How the fuck do you have an operation and not have the ops van nearby? Who the fuck does that? Now, we have to wait and fucking wait and wait some more.

Man, fuck this shit. That joker doin' God knows what to Katie, and I'm sittin' here like a little bitch.

I then see one of the bodyguards carrying the third missing girl, Serenity, from one of the rooms. They're all here. Katie was right.

She was fucking right!

The bodyguard head towards the other door, where Bobby took Katie. This is my chance to help the other two girls. Unfortunately, they looked heavily drugged, so I'll need to work fast to get them out.

Deep down, I know Katie can take care of herself, so she'll need me to help with the others.

And I'll do just that.

I enter what looks like a dressing room and find three women passed out on the floor. Jesus, what have they done to these girls?

I approach the first one, and she's beaten pretty badly but still breathing. So I check on the other two. One has a pulse so light; I can barely register its pulsing. And the other doesn't have a pulse at all.

So, I begin chest compression to get her heart pumping again.

"Come on, you can't die like this, not like this."

I pump her chest several more times when she starts coughing. Finally, I gently roll her to her side, so she can catch her breath, then I feel a sharp pain piercing my shoulder blade. "Fuck, what was that?"

I try to pull whatever it is out of my shoulder when I see the first girl pull a knife out of the very spot I was reaching for. "What the fuck?" I grunt out in pain.

"Fuck you, asshole!" she screams at me. "You're not fucking up what I've worked so hard for. I won't let you!" trying to stab me again. But this time, I catch her arm and twist it, causing the knife to fall and I slam her on the ground hard, knocking the wind out of her.

"Crazy bitch." I then tie her up using my belt.

I search around, hoping to find something to stop the bleeding in my shoulder, when I spot several multicolored silk scarves hanging over one of the dressing room doors. I make my way over, snatch one of them down, and wrap it around my shoulder. I then grab another and make it into a makeshift carrier to hold my arm up. "Damnit!" Well, I certainly can't get both girls out now. I'll have to grab one at a time.

I walk over to one of the girls, "Hey," I shake gently. But in response she groans. "Hey, can you walk?" She shakes her head up and down but doesn't budge. So, with my good arm, I lift her up, hold her by her waist and guide her slowly out of the room.

Several people watch me in either praise or utter disgust. But only one guy come to assist me.

"Hey, do you need help?"

"Yeah, man. I found them passed out, and I believe they need to get to the hospital quick. I've already called for EMS."

"Them? Are there others?" The guy asks.

"Yeah, one is tied up because she attacked me, but the other is in terrible shape. I performed CPR, but she needs help quick."

"Bet; I'll grab the other girl, and we can head to my truck."

"Thanks, man. What's your name?"

"Jake, but you can call me Officer Reek, Officer Henry."

"So, you know who I am?"

"Yep. Worked on a couple of events with you. I come here to relieve some steam, if you know what I mean."

"Yeah, I know. Help should be here in any minute."

"I'll be right behind you." And sure enough, the cavalry arrives and helps me with the girl I'm holding up, barely, and helps Ofc. Reek with the other girl.

"OFFICER, YOU NEED TO COME WITH US SO WE CAN GET THAT shoulder taken care of," an EMS Tech states with concern.

"No, I have to go back in. Others need help."

"But you need help."

"I know. I'll get help as soon as I know they're alright."

"Okay. I know you won't budge. But the moment everything is clear, come see me."

"Deal."

I then find Sgt. Maui and brief her on what has happened, leaving no rock unturned.

"You disobeyed a direct order. I should have your badge for this," she threatens. "However, I understand love. Let's get your woman back," she states more with a softer tone.

And at that moment, I respect the hell out of Sgt. Maui. She's as real as they come.

We head back into the club, ushering everyone out: men, women, and children. One of the officers grabs the crazy bitch out of the dressing room, and I tell them they need to handcuff her. She's the reason I'm stabbed. We then make it to the last room, where Katie is.

As we open the door, Katie has Bobby at gunpoint, the bodyguard has been shot, probably by Katie, and Serenity is being utterly sheltered from harm's way by Katie's body.

My badass firecracker girlfriend and I wouldn't have it any other way.

CHAPTER TWENTY-EIGHT

KATHERINE

SITTING in the hospital's waiting room is the worst shit I've ever had to do. I hate hospitals! Argh! This is for the birds. How can anyone sit here for hours or even days, just waiting? I've got to do something, anything.

As I stand abruptly, I hear my name being called. I turn to find Harper and Dom rushing toward me, and once again, I break into a million pieces. I've f-ing cried more in the past three days than in my entire life.

This isn't me. I don't cry, ever. But here I am, draining every ounce of water I have reserved for, I don't know, hydration, maybe.

Harper crashes into me, and we swing in each other's embrace like long-lost sisters reunited for the first time in years.

She then pulls away and slaps me hard on my arm.

"Ouch! What was that for?" I complain.

"What the hell? You couldn't pick up the fucking phone and tell me what was going on?" she demands.

"No, I wasn't interrupting your honeymoon," I explain.

"Fuck the honeymoon!"

"Whoa, wait a minute there," Dom chastises.

"Dom, you know what I mean," she waves him off.

"Katie, you got a kid?" she questions softly and curiously.

"Yes, but I don't know if it's her. The doctor took my blood to do a DNA test. I'll know in a couple of weeks."

"Seriously, so everything Sgt. Maui briefed me on is true?"

"Define briefed?"

"Bobby is the one that cut you, raped you, and could be the baby's father; well, teenaged daughter, you gave up fifteen years ago. Did I leave anything out?"

"Nope, that pretty much sums it up," I agree sarcastically.

"You've been living with this by yourself all this time?"

"Yeah, pretty much."

"Damnit, Kathrine Nicole Harris. I'm supposed to be your best friend, and you couldn't trust me, trust me enough to confined in me?" she states with hurt in her tone.

"I didn't see it that way. For years, I've felt captive in my own head, and when that video came out, I was literally reliving that nightmare over and over again. I didn't know how to talk about it. Just know, you were part of my healing, keeping my mind off the pain, allowing me to help with the wedding, going to court with you, all of it. It really helped. I just didn't know it at the time."

"Oh, honey, I'm sorry. I'm being very selfish right now."

"You're being you."

"Hey, I resent that."

"Well, it's kinda true," Dom agrees with me.

"No sex for a week," Harper spits out.

"Man, come on, babe. You know I love you either way," Dom whines.

"That's why it's only a week, and not a month," Harper responds.

"Fuck, Katie. You on your own." Dom backs away with his hands up.

"Have you heard anything yet?" Harper asks.

"Jackson is still in surgery, and the missing girls are recovering in their suites."

"Have you spoken to her yet?"

"No, I haven't found the right time to approach her parents."

"Honey, there will never be a right time. You'll just have to do it. She deserves to know the truth."

"I know."

"We'll sit with you until you find the strength, okay?"

"Okay," appreciating the company.

"Do you want anything from the hospital's café?" Dom asks.

"Katie?" Harper offers.

"Yeah, a coffee would be great. Actually, I'll take a red bull. I need something a little stronger on the caffeinated side."

"And I'll take a lemonade," Harper requests.

"I'll be right back." Dom then leaves, and Harper and I sit for what seems forever in silence when a dark-skinned woman approaches us.

"Hi, I didn't mean to startle you; but are you Katherine Harris?" she asks.

"Yes, I am."

"I'm Hilary, Serenity's mom."

"Oh, yes. How is she doing?"

"Considering all she's been through, she's doing wonderful, thanks to you for saving her life."

"Oh, no. I was just doing my job."

"You were being a mom," and my pulse starts to race immediately.

"H—how?"

"She's the spitting image of you," Hilary explains my unspoken question. "She's been asking about you, you know."

"She has?"

"Oh, yes. We explained to Serenity that she was adopted at a very young age. She's always known she had another mom. And when the time came for her to understand, she requested to meet you. Little did we know, we didn't have to look very far."

"She wants to meet me?" I question as Harper squeezes my hand, giving me the comfort I didn't know I needed.

"Yes. Here, listen," she continues as she takes a seat next to me. "We are okay with you being a part of her life if you want. That night when she was given to me, the nurse explained what happened to you. She wanted your baby to have a good home, a better home than you had because you've been through so much. She understood your cries, your concerns, your fears. She didn't want that same fate for your daughter. The nurse is the one who named her Serenity Clarity Rose. I just don't think she knew your real name. But it fit her so well, my husband and I didn't want to change it," Hilary explains.

My voice cracks as I try to respond, and I realize I'm crying again.

"I—I was going through so much. I never even wanted to have her because of how she was conceived. I was forced to have her."

"We know, and we understand. We never resented you for that. She never resented you. We thank you for giving us such a beautiful soul, a well-loved daughter. You saved us. You see, we tried so hard to have children, and that night, when the doctor told us we could never conceive the natural way, I thought my world was over. But, little did we know a miracle was being born, and a gift so precious was given to us. We wanted to meet you that night, but you refused to see anyone, and we wanted to respect your wishes. That's why the nurse explained everything to us. We knew someday; we'd meet the one who gave us hope."

"Oh, God," I cry out. "He was with me! I hated him so much, but he was helping me, saving me all along."

"Yes, and if you're willing, we want you to be a part of our lives."

"Yes, please. I'd love that so much."

Hilary then gives me a loving hug, and all of my fears, doubts, and frustrations evaporate and, in their place, awakens love, hope, and perseverance.

I STAND AT THE DOOR OF MY DAUGHTER'S ROOM, SERENITY Clarity Rose Bostick. As I gaze through the small window, I see her resting peacefully. Wow, she's beautiful. I never took the time before to really look at her. She's the very image of me, to include the scars she's acquired.

She's perfect.

I take a deep breath, decide to stop being a coward, and rip the band-aid off. *You got this, Katie!* Hyping myself up.

I turn the knob, and Serenity turns my way, adjusting her eyes to focus on me.

"Hi, I'm—"

"You're my mom! My biological mom," Serenity finishes my sentence.

"Yes, I'm Katie. How are you feeling?"

"I'm okay, thanks to you."

"Oh, it was nothing. I always do this type of thing," downplaying the situation.

"My mom told me you are a police officer."

"Yes, I've been on the force for over five years."

"Wow, that's pretty cool."

"Yeah, it has its ups and downs."

"I've been trying to find you," she states softly. "That's how me and my friends ended up like this."

"Wh—what? What do you mean?"

"I saw a video of you surfacing the internet. When I saw it, I knew I was related to you. We look too much alike. I convinced my friends to come with me when we found out which club you worked at. We knew it would be a long shot, but when we made it there, Bobby, the owner, stared at me like he was seeing a ghost, and that's when he wouldn't let us leave. But then he did, eventually, and we decided together to never go back, until we were all hunted down. It was like a sick twisted game of his. And when his goons tracked Vivian and Maya; I knew it was only a matter of time before he snatched Emma and me. But we were too scared to tell anyone. I'm so sorry we caused all of this. It's all my fault," Serenity cries.

"No, don't do that. Don't blame yourself. If I never gave you up, you wouldn't be looking for me."

"Mom told me what happened to you. The reason why. That's why I had to find you and tell you that I love you anyway, and what you did; what you went through was the most selfless thing in the world, and I'm proud to have you as my mom."

"And I'm so proud of you," I state fondly because I don't need a DNA test to tell me what's obviously right in my face. This feeling I have is unconditional. No strings attached, no fears in the way. Just pure love, and I wouldn't have it any other way.

"I'd like for you to meet someone, well, when he gets out of surgery," I implore.

"I'd love to get to know all your friends and family!" she gushes. And that's all the validation I need.

"JACKSON," I WHISPER SOFTLY AS I FEEL HIM SLOWING COMING down from the anesthesia.

"Hum," he groans softly.

"It's me, Katie," I whisper.

"Ah, my suga plum," he reaches for me. And, of course, I hear snickering behind me. "Ha, not alone."

"Nope, not alone. I'd like for you to meet someone," I explain.

"Yeeesssss," he slurs.

"Here's my daughter, Serenity."

"Ah, Serenity. Baby girl. Your mama loves you to pieces."

"Yes, I know," Serenity responds.

"Speaking about moms, have anyone called mine? She's going to freak," he burst out laughing.

"I called your sisters. They are all outside. Your dad came, but your mom…well, you know your mom."

"Yep, I sure do. What a heartless, selfish soul," he states softly.

"She'll come around,"

"Doubt it. Hey, Serenity, my casa is your casa."

"Thanks, I think," Serenity laughs.

"Yeah, he's still high as a kite."

"Yep, he is."

Jackson then drifts to sleep, and Serenity and I head out to meet his sisters, brother-in-law, and father. She also meets Harper and Dominique, and this is the best day of my life.

HIS EPILOGUE
JACKSON

ONE YEAR LATER

MAN, that crazy bitch did a number on my shoulder. But, after three surgeries and physical therapy, I finally feel like my old self.

Katie wanted to celebrate my return to work and a reunion for meeting her daughter for the first time.

It's a year later and in the middle of June and hot as hell. Katie and I decided to move in together, so we purchased a home a couple of months ago, with a pool in the back and a huge yard to entertain. She did all of the designing, well, except for my man cave. I drew the line on the bat cave.

So, not only is this a celebration of my return and a reunion for our baby girl, but it's also a housewarming party because Harper insisted that we get things for the house even though it's fully furnished.

After I shower, I head downstairs to link up with Dominique, but I run into Ethan instead.

"Hey, man, nice home," Ethan greets.

"Uh, what are you doing here," obviously puzzled by his appearance.

"Damn, nice to see you too," he state sarcastically.

"I mean, I wasn't expecting you."

"Katie didn't tell you. She invited me. Said she wanted to give me a chance because it's wrong not to accept me, and you've accepted all of her flaws."

"Wow, I wouldn't have never thought in a million years Katie would forgive you."

"You gotta great girl. Hold on to her. She's a keeper."

"Thanks, man, but I must tell you, Dominique will be here."

"I know. She warned me too. Said it's part of my healing and to get my head out of my ass and apologize whether he wants to hear it or not."

"Now, that sounds like my Katie," giving each other some dap.

"You look damn good, man. Healed nicely."

"All Katie doing. That girl, there, is a force to be reckoned with."

"That she is. I'm going to go find Dominique. Catch you later?" he says as he hands me a box.

"Yeah, I'll be here." He then walks away, heading toward the backyard.

I then turn to find Katie. I need her in place and not running around like she always is with events like this.

I make my way to the kitchen when I overhear Sophia Martin, Victoria Morris, Harper, and Katie talking.

"I think you should go for it," Victoria states proudly.

"I don't know, Sophia; he did try to kill me and Dominique last year. I don't think I can trust him like that anymore," Harper admits.

"He's really changed back to the guy I crushed on all those years. I've been checking on him, making sure he's alright. He really needs his friends right now, and I don't know, I think I'm falling hard for him," Sophia divulge.

"Whatever happened to that Derrick guy?" Katie questions.

"Uh, we're just friends. He was helping me with something," Sophia explains.

"Yeah, you never explained what that was," Katie states, patiently waiting for a response. But when she doesn't receive one, Katie continues, "Listen, y'all know how a hard ass I am, but after last year, I've turned a new perspective on everything, so Sophia, if you want to bang Ethan and Derrick, go for it," Katie singsongs. "Life's too short to be afraid of what's to come.

"Yeah, you're right. I really need to tell him that I've forgiven him. Now, I don't know about Dom, but I can say that I have," Harper states. "And Sophia, be careful about your two beaus. Nothing good comes out of playing the field."

"I know Harper, Katie. I know y'all mean well. But, Derrick really is a friend and that's it," Sophia assures.

"Whatever you say," Katie states.

"I'm so proud of you. All of you. Stepping out of your comfort-zone, and taking risks. Y'all rock," Victoria cheers.

"Friends for life!" they all toast with a glass of whatever they're drinking.

That's when I make my entrance, "What smells so good," I ask as I wrap my arms around Katie's waist, pulling her ass against my now-hardened dick. She does it for me every time.

"Hey babe," she coos in my arms. "I've missed you," turning and kissing me like her friends aren't in the kitchen with us.

The lovemaking we created last night and this morning was beyond memorable. Just remembering it got me getting harder by the second. The feel of my dick slipping into my sweet wet, pussy is something I can get with for the rest of my life, and I ain't scared. Not one bit of fear in my bones. Not one bit.

Pushing away the woman I've grown to love more than my own breath was hard, but the next step for my future will be like a breeze on a summer's eve. Just as easy as it comes.

"Harper, can I speak with you for just a moment," glancing her way as I pull away from Katie.

"Yeah, sure. What's up?"

"Love, we'll ensure the grill is at the perfect temperature. You know Harper got the magic touch," I explain to Katie as Harper and I leave the kitchen. "Is everything set?" I ask Harper once we're out of ear shot with a slight hesitation in my tone. This might be the hardest thing I've had to do all my life, yet the easiest.

My sisters, my father, Katie's daughter, and all our friends are here in one setting; why not profess my heart to the only woman I've ever loved? Why not?

"Yes, everything is ready," Harper states with such affirmation. "You know. She's the happiest I've ever seen her. You did that."

"Naw, we did it for each other. She's my rock, my life, my everything."

"I know. I knew two years ago..." she trails off.

"Thank you for allowing me to be her everything," I convey with everything I got. Because I know, Harper is the only one I can ask permission for Katie's hand. She's as close to a family member as she gonna get.

"You're welcome," she utters. "Now, let's get this done before she figures out what we're up to."

"Yes, ma'am."

We make our way into the backyard before Katie can reorganize the entire setup again...

After everyone arrives, the girls bring Katie outside, where Harper has laid yellow rose petals around me. Of course, Katie has no clue what's happening, and I'm grateful to the former Alpha Watch for helping out.

"What's going on out here? Why everyone got their phones out?" Katie surveys the crowd as she joins me. Still oblivious to the rose petals surrounding us. Probably because the breeze is scattering the petals everywhere.

"They're here to witness this," I affirm. I drop to one knee and take Katie's left hand in mine. "Love, Angel, baby girl. You are my everything. I can't breathe without you near me. Hell, I can't think without hearing your voice. And I never want to lose what we have and share, not again. I was physically sick without you and I never want to experience that again. So, will you do me the honor and be my forever love?"

Tears-stricken eyes, Katie hollers at such an incredibly high pitch; it scares the hell out of me and everyone else. "Yes! Yes! Yes!" soothing my confused heart, confirming her love for me.

I lift her up in my arms and spin her around with such passion, and I know she'll always be by my side, no matter what.

HER EPILOGUE

KATHERINE

ANOTHER YEAR LATER

THIS IS the best day ever! My long-lost daughter, Serenity, my best friend, and sister from another mother, Harper and her husband, Dominique, and Jackson's father Mr. Jack, and Jackson's sisters, Jade, Jillian, and Jamie are all here to witness such a wonderful reunion. I couldn't be happier. Unfortunately, his mother has not come around. Oh well, her loss. I no longer have the desire to make people like me.

I never once prayed to be married to anyone, let alone Jackson Henry, but life has a way of changing your entire being for the people you love the most.

I never experienced a love like this before, and yes, I almost lost that too, but Jackson is a force to be reckoned with, blowing straight through my walls with such potency it can knock an ox off its feet.

I tried to ignore him, hell, and it worked for an entire year, but he wasn't havin' it. Not one bit.

Now, it's my turn to be pretty and float down the aisle like Cinderella in that Disney movie. And I will because my husband-to-be spared no dollar for my fairytale wedding.

I really think it has to do with his parents trying to win me over for that shit show of a performance two years ago, but that's in the past now. They know who they dealing with, and I will never be treated as such again, and if they want to be a part of Jackson's life and their future grandchildren lives, they'll get on board, especially his mother. What a piece of work, but that's neither here nor there.

"Honey, are you ready?" Harper asks as she walks into my dressing room of the Mansion. We decided to have the wedding at the Mansion and the reception just across the way in front of the bandshell. It'll be the year's social event, and I couldn't be happier.

"Yes, I'm ready."

I MAKE MY WAY INTO THE HALLWAY, WHERE MY BRIDAL PARTY and Jackson's dad are waiting for me. Mr. Jack was so gracious to walk me down the aisle because my father is nowhere to be found. Once he was released from jail, he never tried to make contact with me, and I have to say, it doesn't bother me not one bit. I have a family. Alpha and Bravo Watch are my family; and now I have Serenity, Jade, Jillian, and Jamie. I couldn't ask for more.

"My dear, you are absolutely breathtaking! That dress is set for a queen," Mr. Jack gushes as I wrap my arm into his.

"Thank you so much for doing this."

"It's not a problem at all. You're family now, and I can see how much my son loves you, and that's all I ever wanted for my children, love, and happiness," he admits, and I can hear the adoration in his voice, more so than I ever have in the short time I've known him, but I feel compelled to take him into a fatherly and daughterly embrace to show my gratitude for his existence. Because if it weren't for him, there would be no Jackson.

"Okay, okay, okay. Enough of the lovey-dovey shit. It took me three hours to get your makeup right. Do not make one ounce of a smudge on that masterpiece, so help me," Sophia chastises. She's been in a shity mood lately, and it's probably got something to do with Ethan.

"Yes, right. Show time!" gathering myself and my thoughts. But I must make sure Sophia is okay first, "Sophia, everything good?"

"Yeah, why do you ask?"

"Well, I don't know, maybe the fact that you're chewing everyone's head off."

"Oh, no. I'm so sorry. It's not you. I promise. I'm just—I'm just dealing with some personal things," she responds, waving me off. "I didn't mean to rub my issues onto everyone else and ruin such a beautiful and memorable moment."

"Nope! Not buying it. Spill the beans," I demand softly.

"Damnit Katie. Why do you do that?"

"Do what?"

"It's Ethan, okay. He's been a little off lately, and I don't know what to do. I've run out of ideas. I want to help so much, but this is beyond my control."

"What's wrong? I thought he was doing better."

"He was, but then Dominique blew him off at the party last year, and he's been angrier and agitated. I'm afraid he may do something."

"Like what?"

"Something to himself," she responds so softly I barely hear her speak.

"What was that?"

"Nevermind. It's your big day. Let's focus on happy things," changing the subject.

"No, tell me. I'm always here for you."

"No," she states firmly.

"Okay, okay, I'll let it go for now," I respond. But we seriously need to sit and talk about this. If Ethan is seriously doing bad, we must step in before he does something he may regret again.

"Ready?" Mr. Jack asks.

"Yep! Let's do the damn thing," and we all burst out laughing as the double doors open to the beautiful aisle created just for this moment, this occasion. Allowing me to forget such a heavy conversation I had with Sophia.

WELL, SO MUCH FOR SOPHIA'S MASTERPIECE. I DIDN'T LAST thirty seconds before the waterworks began to flow, making it extremely difficult to take a glimpse of my knight in shiny armor. And he's just that, simplistically gallant in his gorgeous grey tweed three-piece suit. With his curls styled in a way, I just want to run my fingers through them and ruffle them the way I like.

The moment we say our 'I-do's,' we're one step from creating our own porn movie in front of everyone, probably embarrassing his mom to no end, and guess what? I don't give a fuck, and neither does he. That's what happen when you show the hell up late, trying to be the center of attention...bitch.

Tonight, we will begin adding to our family, and so we do, in the bathroom, the coat closet, and our famous spot in the park by the tennis courts. Where it all began two years ago.

ALSO BY NICOLETTE JOHNSON

Don't forget to indulge in all volumes of the **Handcuffed** Series:

Handcuffed

Shackled

Bounded

Entangled

My Second Series: **Savannah Finest** Series

Alpha Watch

Coming Soon:

Savannah's Finest Series:

Book III

Charlie Watch

Let me know how you like the series thus far

Facebook @authornicolettejohnson

Twitter @PenNicoletteJo

Instagram @authornicolette

www.authornicolettejohnson.com